Councilman Lorian Bakerman knows his mother's dinner invitation is a set-up. Having been dodging her attempts to introduce him to eligible shifter women of her choosing for the last several years, he's learned all the signs. Ever since other single councilmen have begun finding their mates—male mates—she's been urging him to settle down . . . with someone she finds appropriate.

When Lorian accepts a barbeque invitation from Enforcer Germaine for the express purpose of avoiding his mother's plans, he's shocked to find himself drawn in by a pair of sad hazel eyes. Scenting the shifter, he realizes that Randy Cullers is his mate. While Randy acknowledges their connection, he seems timid and uncertain, leaving Lorian confused . . . until he learns that Randy is mourning the loss of a long-standing partner.

Lorian wants Randy and is willing to give him time. Can his patience hold out as he helps Randy's heart mend while stopping his meddling and manipulative mother's ways before she scares him off?

Healing his Forever

ISBN: 978-1-4874-3354-3
Cover art by Angela Waters

Published by eXtasy Books Inc or
Devine Destinies, an imprint of eXtasy Books Inc

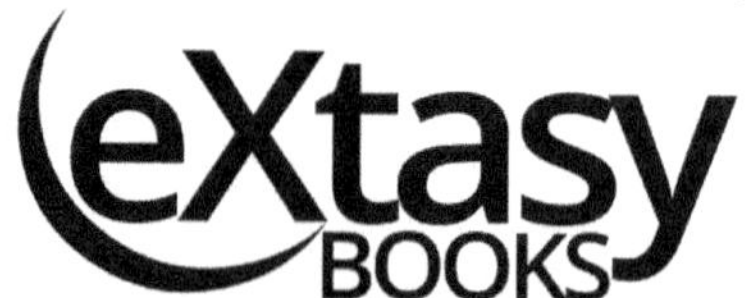

Look for us online at:
www.eXtasybooks.com or www.devinedestinies.com

Healing his Forever
Shifter's Regime: Book Eight

By

Charlie Richards

Dedication

To the simple joy of completing a project. They never end, but the satisfaction is always the same and a reward in and of itself.

CHAPTER ONE

Councilman Lorian Bakerman clicked a button on the computer, saving the file. Opening his email, he sent the information to Alpha Kontra Belikov. He knew the bear shifter would make good use of it.

The prior month, Lorian had met with Kontra, a grizzly shifter and leader of a nomadic biker gang. The man had been hanging around the area while helping a friend settle in with his mate. When Lorian had overheard rumors that Kontra and his people were preparing to move on, he'd asked for a few moments of his time.

While the buffalo Lorian shared his psyche with—or American bison, as some called it—had been a little concerned to be in the same room as a grizzly, Lorian had known he was completely safe. Kontra had come very highly recommended by their Shifter Council's newest member—Shane Alvaro. The wolf shifter and his prior pack had worked with Kontra and his people on a number of occasions.

Besides, Lorian had had Enforcer Dakota Drudeson with him. He knew the Komodo dragon shifter would never have allowed anything to happen to him. While Lorian considered Dakota a friend, it was also the male's job to keep him safe.

Lorian's email pinged, drawing his attention. He spotted a confirmation from Alpha Kontra and smiled. Coordinating with the nomadic gang to clear out facilities they'd found in ex-Councilman Krakow's file—who'd been put to death for his crimes—had been the best decision the council could have made.

Satisfied that Kontra would investigate the tip as soon as he could, Lorian leaned back in his chair and stretched his arms over his head. He arched and felt the soft pop. Grunting with pleasure, he rolled his head slowly on his neck. Once again, Lorian heard and felt a crack.

"Ouch. That sounded like it hurt."

Lorian met Enforcer Germaine's dark-eyed gaze and grinned. "How it sounded is totally different than how it felt," he countered. "Been sitting at this desk for far too long," Lorian admitted as he rose to his feet. When his stomach grumbled a little, too, he glanced at the clock on the wall. "Mmm, missed lunch. How come you didn't holler at me?"

Germaine grinned widely, shrugging his lean shoulders. "You looked like you were in the zone, and I had a big breakfast with Sage," the dark-skinned anaconda shifter told him—referencing his Bengal tiger shifter mate—as he rose to his six-foot-six height. "Ready to head to the cafeteria?"

"I am," Lorian agreed. "I think a massive grilled chicken Caesar salad is calling my name."

Humming, Germaine nodded. "I'm certain a Rueben sandwich is calling mine."

Lorian's stomach growled louder, causing both men to chuckle. Leaving his office, he led the way down the hallway. He noticed Germaine fall into step at his right, the enforcer's gaze always in motion.

While Lorian would have liked to have enough faith in his fellow shifters to call Germaine paranoid, he knew better. There had been too much unrest amongst his kind due to their changing policies. The Shifter Council was finally getting with the times—accepting same-sex fated matings and sending investigators to police pack alphas, removing those who abused their power. Those bigoted and power-hungry shifters who had a hard time with the changes were causing problems. There was no telling where they might strike, which included within the walls of the Shifter Council building itself.

After all, they'd managed to infiltrate it before.

"Are you doing anything for the fourth?"

Arching one brow, Lorian questioned, "The fourth?"

Germaine nodded, his black brows furrowing. "Uh, it's the Fourth of July on Saturday," he reminded him. "A national holiday."

"Oh, right," Lorian murmured, nodding. "Guess I totally lost track of time."

Patting Lorian on the back once, Germaine told him, "You need to get out more, Councilman."

"That's the truth," he agreed with a chuckle.

"Guess that's a *no* on plans," Germaine continued as they reached an elevator. As he punched the *up* button, so they could get to the main level where the cafeteria was, he added, "Sage and I are having a barbeque Saturday afternoon. Bunch of guys who work with the council will be there as well as a few others. You're welcome to join us."

Lorian smiled, unable to remember the last time he'd done something so laid back as a barbeque. At nearly three hundred years old, he'd been a councilman for almost a century. He always seemed to need at least one guard with him.

Of course, a barbeque at an enforcer's home whom I trust . . .

"Well, give it some thought," Germaine continued, telling Lorian that he'd been quiet for too long. "The invitation will still be there."

"I—" The trill of his cell phone interrupted him. When he looked at the screen, he groaned.

Germaine chuckled as he led the way into the elevator. "Maybe you'll lose service in here."

Lorian followed him into the car. "I wouldn't get that lucky," he grumbled before accepting the call. "Good afternoon, Mother."

"Good afternoon, Lorian," Annabelle Bakerman—his

mother—greeted breezily. "How are you today? You're not working too hard, are you? Have you eaten lunch?"

Grimacing, Lorian stated, "I'm fine, Mother. I'm just on my way to lunch now." Before she could respond, he quickly added, "And work is the same as always. Busy." Lorian could guess what his mother would say next, so he told her, "I'm looking forward to a nice, relaxing meal in the sunshine."

"Are you getting another one of those processed meals from your cafeteria again?" Annabelle scolded. She always seemed to have something to complain about. "If you would just settle down with a good woman, you wouldn't have to eat that terrible food."

Knowing Germaine could hear every word that his domineering mother uttered, Lorian tipped his head back and stared at the ceiling. He noticed out of the corner of his eye that the other shifter reached forward and pressed the *stop* button. The elevator ceased its movement, for which Lorian was grateful.

At least no one else will have the chance to overhear her.

"Mother, I've explained before," Lorian began slowly, biting back a sigh of longsuffering. "Our kitchens here are stocked with the finest foods, and the chefs and cooks are top-notch. Anything I get here is fresh and filling." Unable to help himself, Lorian added, "Besides, the food here is free to all shifters and mates. I already employ a chef." Scowling, Lorian muttered, "Why would I ask him to cook me *to go* meals when I can get fantastic food here?"

Lorian had never been so happy as when the microwave had been invented. It had meant he could grill an excessive amount of meat once a week, then reheat it later. Much to his mother's distress, Lorian loved hot dogs and macaroni and cheese.

"If you had a wife, you wouldn't need a chef," Annabelle countered hotly. "She would—"

Unable to help himself, Lorian barked a laugh, cutting her

off.

"Lorian Bakerman," his mother scolded. "How dare you interrupt me. I am your mother."

"My apologies, Mother," Lorian replied by rote. Maybe it was because he knew his enforcer was listening, but he couldn't resist pointing out, "But I doubt any of the women you've introduced me to in the last three years would be able to cook, either."

"Well, you don't know that," Annabelle stated, frost entering her tone. "You refused to give any of them enough of your time to even find out."

"Mother, I've explained this to you." *About a million times.* "I won't lead anyone on. I'm waiting for my fated mate."

Lorian's mother had sporadically tried to set him up for decades. He'd always told her the same thing, not that she listened. Right on cue, Lorian listened to her excuse.

"Well, how are you supposed to meet her if you don't go looking?" Annabelle sounded just as dismissive as always. "If I didn't keep introducing you to people, you would never meet anyone new."

"I meet new people all the time," Lorian replied, rubbing his palm over his neatly trimmed beard.

Gods, I'm so tired of this conversation.

"You meet ruffians and criminals," Annabelle stated with a huff. "No one of good breeding." She sniffed derisively. "Certainly no one worthy of being your fated mate."

"I'm sorry, Mother." Lorian had no desire to hash over the same territory again. "I'm about to get into the elevator, and I'm afraid I might lose you. Can I call you back this evening?"

I'm sure I can come up with an excuse as to why I didn't.

"I hate it when you rush me," Annabelle complained. "I'm holding a Fourth of July dinner party Saturday evening at six. I expect to see you there."

Oh, hell, no. Another set-up.

Seeing Germaine leaning against the elevator wall, his

arms crossed over his lean torso, Lorian had an idea. "I'm sorry, Mother. I've already accepted an invitation to another engagement."

Germaine arched one black brow as the corner of his full dark lips curved up a bit.

"Oh, really?" Annabelle didn't sound convinced. "From whom?" Just as quickly, she demanded, "Have you met someone and didn't tell me?"

"No," Lorian immediately countered. No way did he want his mother to get that idea in her head. "I agreed to a barbeque with a group of friends from work here."

Lorian imagined he could feel the disapproval through the line as the pregnant silence lengthened between them. Holding Germaine's gaze, he asked, "Mother, are you still there?" He didn't expect an answer right away, so he continued, "Damn, must have dropped." Then Lorian disconnected the line. Even as he watched Germaine's lips widen into a shit-eating grin, Lorian stated, "I'm going to hear about that later."

Germaine chuckled as he shook his head. "Damn. Your mother is a little . . ."

The other shifter's voice trailed away, as he seemed to be searching for something that wasn't rude, yet still accurate.

Lorian helped him out. "She's a domineering matriarch." Lorian pressed the button to restart the elevator's movements as he added, "When I became a councilman almost a century ago, I thought it would put some separation between us." Hearing his phone ring, Lorian peered at the screen and shook his head. "It didn't."

Doing something he rarely did, he pressed the silence button. He shoved the phone into his pocket and watched the elevator doors open. It wasn't until they'd both exited and were walking down the empty hallway that Germaine told him, "I won't hold you to what you told Misses Bakerman."

Confused, Lorian asked, "What are you talking about?"

Germaine offered him a wry smile. "The barbeque."

"Oh." Lorian smiled as he shook his head. "I'd actually intended to accept your invitation." Realizing he wasn't completely certain if Germaine had been sincere, he added, "Unless . . ."

Except, how can I ask that without sounding like an ass?

Germaine grinned broadly as he reached around Lorian and grabbed the handle of the swinging doors leading into the cafeteria. "We need to work on our communication, I guess." The man took an obvious glance around before stepping back to let Lorian enter first. "At least, about personal shit."

Lorian chuckled softly. "It's been a long time since I've done something as relaxing as a barbeque," he admitted. "Too much time with"—he grimaced as he joined Germaine at the buffet table—"my mother and her dinner parties."

When did my life become so dull? How did I let that happen?

Even as Lorian wondered, he knew the answers. He'd buried himself in work to avoid his mother's demands as much as possible. That meant when he did make some free time for himself, his mother guilt-tripped him into getting him to do what she wanted.

Gods. Almost three hundred years old, a councilman, and still under my mother's thumb. I'm so lame.

Fortunately, Lorian knew he could do something about it. He knew it wouldn't be easy, but he would. In fact, his refusal of his mother was already a step in the right direction.

Now I just have to stick to my guns and not give in.

"Can I fix you something specific, Councilman Lorian?"

Hearing the melodious tenor pulled Lorian out of his thoughts, and he realized he'd been staring vacantly at the array of food on the buffet. He lifted his gaze and focused on Desmond. The pretty, brown-eyed fox shifter worked in the kitchens. Lorian had heard he was the go-to guy for baked treats, too.

"Hello, Desmond," Lorian greeted with a smile. "Thank you for the offer."

Lorian swept his gaze over the offerings, actually take in what they were real quick before he answered the shifter. When Lorian returned his attention to Desmond's face, he spotted the slight tell-tale flush on his face, and a discreet sniff allowed him to scent the other man's pleasure. Evidently, it pleased Desmond that Lorian knew his name.

Huh. I'm not that stuffy. Am I?

"I'm interested in a grilled chicken Caesar salad," Lorian admitted, glancing at the food again. The only meat he noticed was ham and steak strips. "Is there cooked chicken somewhere?"

"Of course, Councilman," Desmond replied with a nod. "I'll heat some for you and have it out in just a moment." After a glance at the canisters at the end of the line, clearly reading their labels, Desmond nodded. "Good. The Caesar dressing is there."

"Any dried anchovies?" Lorian suddenly asked, thinking adding a few strips to the chicken would taste fantastic.

Desmond hummed, tipping his head to the side. "I'm not actually sure." He nibbled his bottom lip, his scent betraying his worry and concern. "But I'll look."

Lorian didn't want to stress out the cook, so he quickly told him, "It was just a whim, Desmond. Maybe add it to the list for next time if you don't have them." With a grin, he reached for a bowl. "Either way is fine."

Smelling of relief, Desmond nodded. "Yes, Councilman. I'll do that." He turned and headed toward the kitchen door, saying, "I'll be right out with the chicken."

"Thanks, Desmond," Lorian stated as he began filling his bowl with chopped romaine.

Within minutes, Lorian had created a huge Caesar salad for himself. He peered around the room, spotting Germaine sitting with Enforcer Dane and Enforcer Dakota—brothers. After a second of hesitation, Lorian decided to join them. If he was going to Germaine's barbeque, then he figured they would be there, too.

"Good afternoon, gentlemen," Lorian greeted as he sat down next to Dane. "How are you all today?"

"Doing well, Councilman," Dane—the older of the pair—replied. "Germaine says you'll be joining us at his Fourth of July barbeque. Glad to hear it."

As Lorian nodded while placing his napkin over his lap, Dakota grinned, leaning forward. "What kind of beer do you like, Councilman?"

Before Lorian could answer, Desmond appeared at his elbow. "Here you go, Councilman." The fox shifter placed two small plates on the table near him. "I found a few anchovies, after all. This is the last of it, so I'll order more."

"Thank you, Desmond." Lorian smiled up at the shifter. "I appreciate it."

Desmond grinned, his cheeks flushing again, before turning and rushing back to the kitchen.

"He's attracted to you," Dane stated, smirking. "Maybe you should ask him to be your date to the barbeque."

Groaning, Lorian shook his head. "Don't you start, too," he grumbled. "He's not my fated mate, and fucking around with a co-worker would just make it awkward later." Seeing Dane's eyebrows shoot up, Lorian realized just how crass that had sounded. *Oh well.* He turned to Dakota. "And I'm a wine drinker. I'll bring a few bottles."

Lorian turned his attention to adding the meat to his salad, but Dane wasn't done.

"Don't I start, too?" the big shifter pressed. "Someone else trying to set you up?"

"His mother," Germaine revealed.

Upon seeing the questioning looks on the brothers' faces,

Lorian glanced around, then lowered his voice and explained Annabelle's antics.

To his relief, the guys groaned in all the right places, obviously commiserating with him.

Chapter Two

"What are you doing in here?"

Turning from the window, Randy Cullers stared over his shoulder, meeting Sage Kanston's gaze. He forced a smile he didn't feel but couldn't get himself to respond. Instead, he just shrugged his shoulders.

How could he tell his best friend—and former fuck-buddy—that watching all the lovey-dovey antics between the mated couples at the barbeque caused his heart to ache.

Sage crossed to Randy and wrapped his arms around his torso. Resting his chin on Randy's shoulder, Sage hugged him from behind.

Randy sighed and cuddled into Sage's hold. Taking comfort from his friend, he stared out the window some more. The room he'd been hiding in had a fantastic view of the woods.

"Come out and sit with me," Sage encouraged. "Germaine is almost done with the hot dogs. You love hot dogs."

At the mention of hot dogs, Randy's stomach growled. "You know me so well," he murmured, smiling for real, just a little. "I'd love a couple of hot dogs. Is there relish and onions?"

"Of course," Sage replied, although he didn't ease his hold quite yet, which Randy appreciated. "Is there any other way to doctor a hot dog?"

Randy chuckled softly, appreciating Sage's teasing humor. Just a few short months before, the tiger shifter had fucked him on a semi-regular basis. He would join Randy and Cain every month or so for a night of three-some fun.

That had all changed on a dime just the month before.

Sage had met his fated mate, Germaine, a male anaconda shifter. Prior to that, all of them had believed that Fate didn't grant same-sex mates. They'd learned that their skulk alpha had been lied to by the aid of Councilman Peregrine—an owl shifter named Cranston Burgess. The man had been doctoring reports to hide that fact, but he was now in custody.

From what Randy had overheard, Enforcer Delanrue had enjoyed torturing Cranston to extract every ounce of information that he could from him.

Randy had cringed upon hearing Germaine's cold, husky chuckle. The anaconda shifter could be damn scary sometimes. Still, he was a wonderful mate to Sage, so he kept his opinion to himself.

Pushing thoughts of the past aside—there was no point in dwelling on his lost relationship—Randy straightened. He pulled away from Sage and smiled at the larger man. "I'll be okay."

Sage nodded, squeezing his shoulder. "I know you will." Looping his arm through Randy's, he urged him toward the door. "It'll just take time."

"Time," Randy repeated, nodding.

After a second of hesitation, Sage whispered, "Have you heard from Cain recently?"

Randy's gut twisted at the mention of his ex-partner. After Sage had mated with Germaine and revealed that Fate did pair those of the same sex, Cain had met his own fated mate. The guy had been a human working as a long-haul trucker. Even as it had broken his heart, Randy had encouraged Cain to travel with the man. Otherwise, Cain wouldn't have seen him again for several weeks.

Shaking his head, Randy admitted, "I asked him not to call me."

"Really?" Sage sounded surprised. Then he sighed as he

nodded. "I understand. You were together for over thirty-three years. I'm sure hearing his voice wouldn't help with moving on."

"Exactly," Randy whispered sadly.

Cain had called Randy the evening after he'd left. His ex-lover had been worried about him, which was nice. Unfortunately, Randy had been able to hear Cain being kissed by his mate. Then, when the man had asked who Cain was talking with, his ex had called him *a good buddy*.

It had been gut-wrenching. Randy had known a clean break was for the best.

Now I just have to figure out how to sleep through the night without Cain's arms around me.

More than once, Randy had woken up reaching out, trying to find his ex in his sleep. Crying himself back to sleep always sucked. He woke the next morning with a headache and a stuffy nose.

While Sage never said anything, Randy knew his friend worried about him. He just felt grateful that Germaine allowed him to sleep in his spare room. The possessiveness of mated pairs had surprised Randy.

Before Randy even reached the back door, he heard the rumble of many voices. He paused at the sliding door and stared at all the people milling around the deck and backyard. Men held red cups, beer bottles, and wine glasses. They stood or sat at a couple of tables, talking and laughing. There were a few that were obvious couples, but not nearly as many as Randy had feared.

Germaine stood at the grill with a blond-haired man holding a platter. Sage's lover was busy filling it with hot dogs and hamburger patties. The blond laughed at something Germaine said, making his green eyes twinkle.

"Come on," Sage urged. "I'll introduce you around." With a wry smile, he added, "I think I remember everyone's names."

Randy snickered, feeling true mirth for the first time in . . . what felt like forever. Opening the door, he allowed Sage to guide him outside. His senses were immediately assaulted by the scents of grilling meat. His stomach rumbled in anticipation, and his mouth watered appreciatively.

"Oh, yum," Randy whispered. "That smells so good."

He hadn't realized he'd been so hungry.

Sage grinned. "It really does."

"Hey, Randy," Germaine greeted with a smile even as he swept an assessing gaze over him. "You're just in time."

"If it tastes half as good as it smells, I'm going to eat until I pop," Randy claimed, rubbing his hand over his belly.

"Well, we sure have plenty." The blond held out his hand. "I'm Dakota Drudeson." As soon as Randy took the shifter's hand, Dakota waggled his brows and stated, "So nice to meet you, cutie."

Germaine scoffed as he closed the lid to the grill and set down his tongs. "Hmmm . . ." Wrapping his arm around Sage, he tugged him against his side as he glanced between Randy and Dakota. "I suppose Dakota wouldn't make a bad rebound fuck." He lifted one slender shoulder in a half-shrug. "He's supposed to be good in bed, or so he boasts."

"Damn right, I am." Dakota rested his left hand on Randy's hip and winked. "And I'd be happy to help in any way you need."

Randy felt his face heat, and he knew he blushed. Doing his best to ignore it, he eased his hand free of the other man's. "When I'm ready for that, I'll be sure to keep you in mind."

Dakota grinned broadly. "I hope so, cutie. I hope so." Then he picked up the platter from where he'd set it on a nearby stool beside the grill at some point. "I'll move these to the table. You hungry, Randy?"

Nodding, Randy looked Sage's way, but he was busy being kissed by Germaine. Dakota must have noticed, too, for he laughed and wrapped his arm around Randy's shoulders. The hold was loose, companionable, so Randy didn't try to get away when Dakota started them both toward a long table laden with all kinds of food.

"How are you liking Georgia?" Dakota asked in a friendly manner. "You're originally from Massachusetts, like Sage, right?"

Evidently, Sage hadn't shared his and Randy's history with anyone. He was just fine with that. "I am," he confirmed. "I just got out of a long-standing relationship and needed a change." Randy decided to leave it at that. "Since Germaine was moving Randy here, he offered me his spare room." As Randy picked up a plate, he added, "I admit I haven't seen much of the area. I've been having fun running around in fox form, though."

Life is simpler as a fox.

"Ah." Dakota released his shoulders and placed the platter in an open area of the table near the bags of buns. "Change is hard, but having a support system makes all the difference." Smiling at Randy, Dakota grabbed the bag of hamburger buns. "Want one?"

Randy shook his head. "I'm going for the hot dogs," he revealed, picking up that bag instead.

Dakota hummed as he took two buns. "Nice. We have all the fixin's. Germaine doesn't do anything by halves."

"It all looks amazing," Randy stated, for want of something to say.

Then Randy took two hot dog buns, closed the package, and set it back down. He doctored his buns with mayonnaise, mustard, and ketchup. After placing the dogs in the prepared buns, Randy added relish and onions.

Randy looked over all the possible side dishes, and he decided simple comfort food was all he needed. Popping the top on a canister of French onion *Pringles*, Randy poured a pile of them onto his plate beside the dogs. After closing the container and putting it back on the table, he grabbed the serving spoon in a massive bowl of macaroni and cheese and helped himself to a couple of scoops.

"Let's find a table," Dakota offered, bumping Randy with his arm. "I'll introduce you to whoever stops by."

"Oh, um." Randy looked Sage's way again, but he didn't see him.

"Sorry about Sage ditchin' ya." Dakota must have followed where Randy was looking. "They're newly mated, and Sage walked outside with your scent on him." He smirked and rolled his eyes. "I'm guessing Germaine felt the possessive need to replace your scent with his own."

Parting his lips in surprise, Randy nodded absently. He'd seen the pair slip away plenty of times over the last few weeks.

Especially any time Sage gave me a nice comforting hug.

"That sounds about right," Randy murmured. Giving Dakota a small smile, he nodded. "Okay."

"Come on." Dakota stopped at a couple of coolers. "Beer, wine, or other?"

"Um, white wine, if possible."

Dakota nodded. "Sure. Sit at the table here, and I'll get it from the kitchen." Then he started toward a nearby table.

"Oh, I can have something else," Randy countered, not wanting to put the nice shifter out. "Juice. Water. Whatever's in the cooler."

Chuckling, Dakota shook his head. "Don't worry about it, Randy." He placed his food in front of a chair. "I think the councilman is ready for a refill, too, so I'll just bring the bottle."

Following where Dakota pointed, Randy just about swallowed his tongue. He spotted a tall, broad-shouldered man who appeared to be in his mid-to-late forties. For some reason, the image of the man rubbing his neatly trimmed beard over Randy's shaved groin popped into his head.

Randy yanked his gaze away from the councilman, fighting back the heat that suddenly began to permeate his body. To his shock, arousal swam through his veins. He even began to plump up—something he hadn't done since Cain had left him.

Thoughts of his ex eased his arousal somewhat.

"Think he's pretty hot, huh?" Dakota rumbled softly, patting his shoulder. "I'll introduce ya."

Before Randy could decline, Dakota headed away from him. He quickly pulled out a chair and sat in it. His gut churned for a new reason—uncertainty. Randy couldn't ever remember getting boned up from just a brief glance at a guy.

Randy watched covertly as Dakota headed not toward the councilman, but toward the house. Sighing in relief—*definitely not disappointment*—he picked up a chip and popped it into his mouth. Chewing slowly, Randy hummed at the delicious flavor.

Starting on a hot dog next, Randy took a big bite. He sighed in contentment. The comfort food was just what he needed.

Unable to help himself, Randy found his gaze straying across the yard. The man Dakota had indicated was talking to another blond man. The hand not holding an empty wine glass was shoved into the pocket of his designer jeans, stretching the fabric over the fly of his groin. Even from a distance, Randy could see that the councilman was well-endowed.

Typical of a shifter. Yum!

Ugh! I should not be thinking about him, or anyone, like that. I'm not ready.

Besides, Dakota had said the man was a councilman. There was zero chance the man would want to date a bottom-boy twink like him. The councilman would need some buff guy or socialite woman on his arm. Someone of good breeding and standing in the shifter society.

Randy knew he was a no-one.

Just as Randy had shoved the last bite of his hot dog into his mouth, the councilman looked his way. The man pinned Randy with a rich, chocolate-brown-eyed gaze. Randy quickly lowered his focus to his plate and grabbed his napkin. After wiping his fingers and his mouth, he picked up his spoon and took one bite after another of his mac and cheese.

So good.

"Here's your wine, Randy."

Dakota's voice pulled Randy out of his singular focus on his food. He saw the glass as well as the bottle the other shifter placed before him. The label read a white zinfandel he didn't recognize.

"Thank you," Randy murmured, reaching for the glass.

"Hey, Councilman Lorian," Dakota greeted, causing Randy to freeze, his fingers wrapped around the stem of the glass. "Ready for a refill?" Grinning, he pointed at the table. "You don't mind me bringing it out, do you? Chow's ready, too."

"No, I don't mind at all, Dakota," a deep baritone voice replied. "And I told you. Call me Lorian when we're not at the office."

Dakota chuckled. "That'll take some getting used to, Lorian."

"I imagine so."

Randy peered at the councilman—Lorian—from beneath his lashes. His breathing hitched as he met the other shifter's deep brown eyes. The man's eyes narrowed just a smidge as he openly inhaled deeply.

Then the corners of his lips curved into the smallest of smiles.

"While I told you that anyone was welcome to try the case of wine I brought, I have to say"—Lorian's deep voice caused goose bumps to break out on Randy's arms—"the fact that you're offering it to my mate pleases me to no end."

"Your mate?" Dakota's voice was full of surprise. "Randy

is your mate?"

Randy's breath caught in his throat.

I'm his mate?

Then Lorian's scent finally registered, and Randy bit back a whimper at the delicious masculine goodness emanating from the man.

Holy shit.

Lorian reached out and used crooked forefingers under Randy's chin to urge him to meet his gaze fully. "Your name is Randy?"

Instead of answering Lorian's question, Randy blurted out what he'd been thinking just a few minutes prior.

"I'm not ready for a mate."

Chapter Three

Only Lorian's self-discipline kept him from rearing back as if slapped. He did lower his hand, however, his fingers threatening to twitch from the faint remembered touch to the other half of his soul. He knew the young male before him was a shifter—some sort of canine, if he didn't miss his guess. There was no reason Lorian could think of for a shifter to deny his fated mate.

"Oh, Randy," Dakota rumbled, shaking his head. His expression appeared sad. "Fate brings mates together when they need each other most."

The big blond settled in a chair beside the younger shifter and touched his shoulder. That drew Randy's attention away from Lorian, which he didn't like in the least, but as he saw his mate's attention move to Dakota, he saw something within the depths of his pretty, hazel eyes that he'd somehow missed—fear and pain.

Something happened to my mate.

"This is a fantastic thing," Dakota continued. "Don't say something you can't take back."

"I—" Randy began before nibbling his bottom lip, ceasing whatever he'd intended to say. Peering at Lorian through his lashes, he whispered, "I'm sorry. I-I didn't mean it . . . like that."

Lorian nodded once. "Very well."

He glanced at Randy's food-laden plate, and his stomach rumbled. Originally, he'd walked over for the food, but he'd detoured when he'd spotted Dakota with the bottle of wine.

Then, scenting Randy had derailed every other thought in his head.

Deciding Randy needed a second to come to grips with this turn of events—truth be told, so could Lorian—he decided to grab a plate of chow for himself.

After all, the hot dog and mac and cheese looked fantastic.

Needing to touch again, Lorian cupped Randy's jaw, brushing his thumb under the pretty man's lower lip. "I'll get food," he declared. "Then we can sit and talk."

Lorian didn't wait for confirmation. After one more gentle swipe under Randy's plump lip—lips he had every intention of tasting by the end of the night—he released the man. Lorian crossed to the food table and began preparing himself a plate.

Out of the corner of his eye, Lorian watched Randy. He didn't really think the shifter would flee, but he couldn't help but watch him. The man was just too pretty not to be admired.

Randy sported a lithe frame—a runner's build, some called it—that would fit perfectly in his much brawnier arms. Lorian hoped Randy kept his ear-length, dark-brown hair that same length or longer because it would be perfect to tuck behind his ears before kissing him or to grip while fucking him. His smooth skin begged for Lorian to rub his calloused hands over it.

"You're sure?"

Lorian jerked his gaze to the left, finding Germaine standing next to him. He didn't miss the fact that the guy had disappeared for a few minutes. The shifter was now drenched in Sage's scent, and the smell of sex still clung to his skin.

"Yes." Lorian wasn't going to pretend he didn't know exactly what the enforcer meant. The news was probably all over the barbeque already. "Randy is my mate. How do you know him?"

Considering Randy was at Germaine's barbeque, he had to know the guy fairly well.

"Randy is a good friend of Sage's," Germaine told him, picking up a plate of his own to fill. "He didn't know Fate paired those of the same sex, so he settled down with a partner"—pausing, he looked Lorian in the eye—"who found his own mate last month. We offered him a room while he recovered from . . . losing his lover of over thirty-three years." Germaine cleared his throat, an uncomfortable expression creasing his features. "I'm sure you'll find out eventually, but, uh—" He rubbed the back of his neck as he leaned close and whispered, "Randy and Sage used to hook up before we bonded. I wanted you to know upfront, so you didn't think he was trying to hide anything from you . . . especially since he's staying here right now."

Even as a surge of possessive jealousy ripped through him, Lorian kept his features neutral. He could understand why Germaine would share that with him. A shifter could get a little . . . volatile . . . if they thought their claim was in question.

Lorian took a deep breath, then let it out through pursed lips. Meeting Germaine's gaze, he nodded once. "Thank you for telling me." As Lorian began finishing up his choices—chili cheese dogs with onions, macaroni and cheese, and potato salad—he asked, "Will you and Sage join us while we eat? It may make him more comfortable."

Germaine nodded. "I'll get Sage." He paused, then shook his head. "He's already there. I'll just bring our food," he amended with a chuckle.

Returning his focus to the table, Lorian saw that Sage had indeed joined Randy and Dakota. Dane was sitting at the table, too. Lorian felt the hairs on his neck stand on end as he saw his unbonded mate sitting with two other unmated shifters.

Damn, these urges are unfamiliar.

As Lorian returned to the table, he realized his decision to deny his mother and hang out with the enforcers had been the best one of his life. Thoughts of his mother calmed some of his eagerness. He knew the woman would raise hell when she realized his fated mate was not only a man, but what she would call a gold-digging commoner.

"Hello, gentlemen," Lorian greeted the others with a smile as he placed his food before the chair to Randy's right. He appreciated that they'd been wise enough to leave it free. As Lorian settled on it, he focused on Randy. "Hello, my mate." Once his hands were free, Lorian held out his right one to Randy. "I'd like to officially introduce myself. I'm Lorian Bakerman. Please, call me Lorian . . . or mate."

Randy swallowed so hard that his Adam's apple bobbed. Still, he reached out and took Lorian's hand. "Randy Cullers," he whispered.

Lorian lifted Randy's hand to his lips and kissed the back of it. "So very pleased to meet you, Randy." Only knowing that they needed both hands to eat gave him enough control to release him. He pointed at Randy's plate and the remnants of his meal. "A man after my own heart. Are those chips good?"

As Randy nibbled his bottom lip, he nodded. Lorian didn't miss the way Sage nudged Randy's arm. When Randy looked the shifter's way, Sage nodded in an encouraging way.

When Randy refocused on Lorian, he smiled at his mate. "Shall we eat and share a little about ourselves?" Then he focused on Dane and Dakota. "I'm confused as to why you're here."

Dane cradled his beer in one hand as he scooped up a forkful of pasta salad with his other hand. Before shoveling the food into his mouth, he rumbled, "You found your mate. You're not bonded. You both need a round-the-clock bodyguard."

Dakota pointed at Randy. "I'm his." He pointed at Dane. "Dane is yours." Grinning widely, he added, "Self-appointed, of course." Then Dakota winked, "And congratulations, Lorian."

Even as Lorian understood the necessity of it, having an audience while he tried to woo his mate was . . . annoying.

Dane probably read his expression, for the shifter told him, "It's just when you're out in the open like this." He indicated the large backyard, which backed to forestland. "When you're in your homes, we'll keep our distance."

Turning back to find Randy staring between the brothers with wide eyes, Lorian reached over and touched his wrist. "I'm sorry, Randy." To his pleasure, the move drew Randy's focus back to him. "There are certain . . . security issues that have to be met when you're bonded with someone on the Shifter Council."

Randy nodded slowly, his eyes filled with concern. "Are you really in danger?" Then he frowned. "Would I be in danger, too?"

Just the idea of Randy in danger caused Lorian's buffalo to bellow in his mind. Before he could figure out the best way to reassure his mate, Dane responded.

"It's a possibility, Randy," Dane told him seriously. "There have been a lot of changes over the last decade, and not every shifter is happy about them." Focusing on Lorian, he added, "Another councilman finding his mate in a man is going to rile a few feathers"—he grimaced—"including your mother's."

Lorian growled softly, even as he knew that Dane was right. "She can go to hell in a handbasket and take her bigoted views with her."

Dakota barked a laugh, grinning broadly as he picked up his bacon-cheeseburger. "I would so love to be a fly on the wall if you ever decide to actually say that to her." Then he took a big bite, a smile still curving his lips.

Understanding, Lorian focused on carefully picking up his

chili cheese dog. "So, how old are you, Randy?" he asked with interest before taking a bite.

"I'm fifty-eight," Randy replied while scooping up a spoonful of mac and cheese. "What about you?"

Pleased to be able to talk about something so mundane—and Randy's young age explained why he appeared to be in his mid-twenties—Lorian quickly swallowed and admitted, "I'm two-hundred-ninety-three." Knowing he had to come clean, he added, "It's been a lot of years since I've been with a man, but I remember I prefer being the top."

Gods, I hope that doesn't end up causing problems.

Sage chuckled as he nudged Randy's upper arm with his elbow. "That totally works for you, doesn't it, Ran?" He winked as he looked Lorian's way. "Randy is a total bottom-boy."

"Say it a little louder, why dontcha," Randy grumbled, his face and neck pinking.

Even as Lorian appreciated the information, he wished he was finding it out in a more private setting. He glanced around, surprised to see that most of the other guys were keeping their distance. They'd moved some tables around, so they could eat a good thirty-plus feet away near the back of the yard. Of course, with shifter hearing, there was no guarantee that was far enough away, but they all seemed more interested in their own conversations rather than what was going on at Lorian's table.

That's nice of them.

"Anyway. I'm glad Fate took care of that for us," Lorian began, trying to move the conversation forward. He smiled at the man he hoped to soon make his lover. "You mentioned you're not ready to meet your mate." Seeing Randy's nod while once again nibbling his bottom lip, Lorian told him, "I'm almost three centuries. I'm a patient man, Randy. Is this because of"—he glanced at Germaine, who was in the process of putting plates before Sage and the final empty chair at the table—"your ex?"

Randy dropped his spoon on the table and wrapped both hands around the stem of his wineglass. "Geez, nothing is private with you two around." He cut a frown Sage and Germaine's way before glaring at his wine glass. "Yeah. I was with this guy for just over thirty-three years. Cain." Randy flicked his gaze at Lorian before taking a sip of his wine. "We didn't think Fate gave gay people a mate, and we fell in love." Shrugging, he admitted, "When we found out, we still didn't plan to separate, but we also vowed never to stand in the way of the other if our fated mate did come along." Scoffing, Randy mumbled, "Two days later . . ."

While Lorian felt jealous as hell that another man held Randy's heart, he did his best to hide it. He prayed to whichever god cared to listen that, soon, he would replace Cain there.

And if not replace, then be able to share.

Lorian had always known that Fate paired both men and women. He'd never bothered to counter a couple of ex-councilmen's views, and he realized that Fate had been punishing him for it. Besides, Lorian considered himself bisexual, so he'd figured his own mate would be female.

His apathetic attitude had had a detrimental impact on his people.

Now that I'm helping with change, I'm being blessed. I just have to patiently woo my mate.

"I'm sorry we didn't ferret out Cranston's lies long ago." Lorian wiped his left hand on a napkin, then laid that palm over one of Randy's wrists. "I don't know if it would have changed anything with you to know you had a fated mate waiting, but I'd like the chance to get to know you. To go on dates and learn each other's likes and dislikes." With a smile he hoped didn't seem pushy, he added, "I know you're safe in this home with Germaine, but please allow Dakota to keep you safe when we're at work."

Lorian waited, albeit impatiently as Randy glanced from his hand to Sage to the others around the table, then back to his wine. He didn't know what he would do if his mate refused him. His instinct to care for, please, and keep Randy safe were already flaring . . . and they pulled him in several directions.

How I wish I could toss Randy over my shoulder and take him home with me. I'd tie him to my bed and pleasure him until he could think of no other's touch but mine. I wish to sink my cock deep into his lean body and feel his heat wrapped around me.

I–

A light kick to his right leg yanked Lorian out of his lustful thoughts. He snapped his gaze right and spotted Dakota's smirk as he rubbed his nose.

Realizing he was hard as nails and probably pumping out all kinds of arousal pheromones, he inhaled deeply, trying to calm himself. Unfortunately, that didn't help much. All he could smell was his mate's breathtaking aroma mixed with his food. For some reason, Randy and his favorite comfort foods mixed together created the headiest aroma . . . ever.

Randy blew out a breath, and Lorian met his gaze. He watched his mate shift a little in his chair. His cheeks were flushed, and from his scent, Lorian knew it was for a whole new reason.

He's just as aroused as I am. Thank fuck!

Lorian felt certain he wouldn't be able to act on it, yet. Still, knowing he affected Randy so gave him hope. To Lorian's relief, so did his mate's softly spoken words.

"I do feel the mate-pull." Randy met Lorian's gaze beneath his lashes. "I understand we're mates. Um, yeah. I like the idea of dating a little first." Rubbing his forefinger over the stem of his wineglass, Randy whispered, "I don't mean to make you jump through hoops, but I need a little time to come to grips with . . . everything."

Gently, Lorian slid his hand up Randy's wrist to his hand.

He gently tugged it free of the stemware. Turning it, he pressed a kiss to Randy's palm.

"I'll give you all the time you need, my mate."

Gods, I hope I can make good on that promise.

Chapter Four

Randy couldn't remember the last time he'd been more nervous . . . or confused. Sitting on the sofa in his friends' front room, waiting for Lorian to pick him up for their date, he rubbed his palms over his thighs uneasily. He knew it was irrational, but he couldn't help himself.

"I hope ya don't mind me sayin' it," Dakota piped up from a nearby loveseat. He'd been reading something on his phone, but now he was looking at Randy. "But you seem as nervous as a cat in a room full of rocking chairs. What gives?" Cocking his head, Dakota continued, "Aren't you excited about your date with Lorian?"

"Yes," Randy answered before nibbling his lower lip uncertainly. "But he changed it to a double date. Why would he do that? Doesn't he want to be alone with me?" Groaning, Randy heard how ridiculous that sounded. Still, he whined, "I haven't been on a date in decades. I don't remember how to act anymore."

Dakota leaned forward, his forearms resting on his thighs. "Did you ask him why he changed it to a double date?"

Randy grimaced, shaking his head. "When he called after getting home last night, I just agreed." Scoffing softly, he mumbled, "Guess I was just so surprised that he actually called like he said he would."

After they'd finished eating at the barbeque, they'd sat around chatting a little. He'd answered questions posed to him, but he struggled to think of any of his own. He appreciated that Lorian willingly shared information with him.

Lorian told him what it was like growing up a couple of centuries before. Things had been easier and harder in a number of ways. His buffalo herd had been farmers, working the land from dawn to dusk. Lorian's herd had even occasionally used their buffalo forms to draw the plow.

As technology progressed, Lorian had known they had to stop that practice and change with the times. They'd had a man in their herd who'd ended up a wiz with finances, but their alpha hadn't wanted to adjust. Lorian had challenged him and won, then began to change policies. His herd-member had invested their funds early in computers. While they'd continued to farm, it hadn't been how they'd made their living.

When an opening on the Shifter Council for what was considered a prey animal shifter had opened, his beta had put in Lorian's name. Lorian had been surprised, but flattered. He'd been even more shocked when he'd been elected into office.

The way Lorian had blushed and admitted that it was probably due a lot to his beta and his mother's campaigning abilities had been sweet. He'd been on the council for over ninety years. Due to the scandal created by the ex-councilmen who'd been selling shifters, they currently had an opening for a predator shifter, and they were sorting through applications.

Lorian had explained the process, and Randy hadn't thought it sounded too complicated. It just sounded lengthy. Each person had to be met with and vouched for by two existing councilmen. Then a number of meetings needed to be held to see how they would mesh with everyone.

When Randy had expressed his view, Lorian had chuckled. He'd squeezed his hand and nodded. "You wouldn't think so, would you?" Then he'd sobered and told him, "Unfortunately, we're getting a lot of applications from people none of us have ever heard of. With the unrest, it's difficult to know who to trust. We have to send in an investigator to each pack or pride first, covertly, to learn about the shifter on the application as well as their loyalty ties." With a wince, Lorian admitted, "That has to be done for our safety before we send a councilman to meet with the shifter. Sadly, many of the investigators come back with horrific tales of abuse, and we have to send enforcers in to clean up the pack." Lorian's expression had turned appalled as he whispered, "Some of the reported conditions . . ." He shook his head. "I don't know how we allowed things to get so bad out there."

"We're overworked and understaffed," Dane had commented, frowning. "We don't have enough enforcers to clean up packs and to escort a councilman to meet a candidate who is part of a good pack."

Germaine had sighed deeply and grumbled, "It's a bit of a mess right now."

"Long hours," Lorian stated with a grimace. Then he'd snapped his focus back to Randy. "But I will make time for you. How about a late lunch date tomorrow?"

Randy had hesitated only an instant before he'd agreed.

Lorian had left shortly after that, once again kissing his palm. As the buffalo shifter had promised, he'd called once he'd gotten home and settled in bed. Then he'd shared the change in plans—having another councilman and his mate join them, making it a double date.

"Why didn't you think he would call?" Dakota asked curiously. "He's your mate."

Drawn out of his thoughts, Randy again focused on his new friend and protector. *So very weird.* "I know he's my mate." Randy smiled a little. "My fox is totally enamored with him and wants to rub all over him. It's a strange sensation."

While Randy and Cain had run and played together in fox form, their animals had felt like brothers, loving each other as pack-mates. They hadn't been enamored with each other. Randy could definitely feel a difference.

"And I don't know why I was surprised," Randy admitted with a shrug. "He's a big powerful councilman." He waved at himself. "I'm just me. A nobody." Recalling words that Lorian had let slip, Randy added, "His mother is totally going to point out our differences in status. What if he comes to resent me just because Fate decided we should be together?"

Dakota sighed deeply, relaxing back on the sofa. "I can't see that happening. Sure, Lorian is a councilman, but he also remembers pulling a plow in animal form. He comes from humble roots, and he remembers that." Scoffing, Dakota curled his lip. "Even if his entitled mother doesn't." Softening his expression, he stated, "You are his mate, he is almost three hundred years old, and he's been waiting for you for a long damn time. He's grateful, Randy. Don't lose sight of that."

Randy nodded, not knowing how to respond to that. After his lover had left, he'd had so many uncertainties arise. He hadn't realized he'd felt so inadequate.

Fortunately, the sound of a large engine saved Randy from having to come up with anything. He rose to his feet, unable to stay still any longer. Giving in to curiosity, Randy moved to the window's edge and began lifting the curtain.

"Whoa, whoa." Dakota was at his side instantly, stopping him. When Randy frowned questioningly at him, Dakota explained, "Learn to check windows discreetly, from the shadows. That way, after you bond with Lorian, you won't be putting yourself or him in jeopardy when you're not in a secure location."

Randy's gut clenched as his heart began to race. "Is it really that dangerous for him?"

Dakota smiled. "I like that you immediately thought of his safety first." The big shifter squeezed his shoulder, the gesture feeling reassuring to Randy. "It depends on the day, to be honest. Right now, things are pretty quiet, but that can change. Form the habits now."

Licking his lips, Randy nodded. "That makes sense." He returned his focus to the window and asked, "Will you show me what you mean?"

Nodding, Dakota stepped to the side. Then he carefully tugged the curtain away from the pane. "Stay off to the side, and stay in the shadows." He released the curtain and stepped away, allowing Randy to take his place. "If you want to check the other direction, you cross to the other side of the window and do the same."

Randy followed Dakota's instructions, but all he saw was the expansive front lawn. Crossing to the other side, he peeked that way. He saw the driveway and an unfamiliar SUV parked there. Dane stood near the back, opening the door.

As Randy watched, he saw Lorian slip out. His breath caught in his chest as he took in his mate. He looked absolutely breathtaking in form-fitting designer jeans and a pale-blue polo shirt that clung to his torso in all the best ways. A light breeze ruffled his short, dark-brown hair, and Randy's fingers itched to feel if it was as soft as it looked.

Oh, wow. These urges sure hit fast and hard. No wonder Cain looked so shell-shocked when I came home that day.

Even as Randy's heart panged a smidge at thoughts of Cain, he realized they weren't as painful as they had been. Instead, anticipation beat out the familiar sadness. He'd thought his relationship with Cain had been fantastic, even if they did have to have an occasional third to fulfill his lover's desire to be fucked.

Now, I know better. Seeing the bond between fated mates is so very different.

Randy eased away from the window and moved to the middle of the room. He stared at the front door. As tempting as it was to yank open the door and meet him on the lawn,

Randy refused to give in to the urge.

He wanted to be picked up like a real date. Plus, he wasn't certain if Lorian would appreciate that kind of eagerness. He didn't know how demonstrative his date would be. Holding hands in the backyard with a bunch of your friends was one thing. Having a guy cling to you in the front yard, for anyone who might be driving by or looking out their windows to see, was something else altogether.

Still so much to learn about him.

Randy knew that if Sage had been there, he would have said something witty to make him laugh and help him relax. Too bad his friend had already agreed to help paint Miggs's living room. Evidently, the newly mated guinea pig shifter hadn't been a fan of Delanrue's home's décor. Miggs was redecorating the whole place. Originally, Randy had planned to help, too, but both men had assured him that a date with his mate took total precedence.

The knock on the door was expected, and Dakota answered it. "Good afternoon, Lorian." With a grin, the blond backed up and swept his hand toward the right. "Your young hottie awaits."

Lorian growled at Dakota as he entered the house. "Find your own young hottie," he ordered. "Randy is mine."

Dakota laughed as he lifted his hands in placation. "I'm trying, sir. I'm trying." Then he backed up a few steps. "And I know he's yours."

After frowning at Dakota for another few seconds, as if making certain he'd gotten his point across, Lorian turned toward Randy. His expression immediately melted into one of appreciation. His deep brown eyes glimmered as he looked Randy up and down, and he stalked toward him.

Randy suddenly felt as if he were prey, even though technically he was a fox and his mate was a buffalo.

Wow. I think of him as my mate already.

"Hello, Randy, my mate," Lorian rumbled, his voice husky

and intimate. Reaching out, he rested his hands on Randy's shoulders. "You look absolutely stunning."

Lorian gently caressed the sides of Randy's neck with his thumbs, causing the hairs on his nape to stand on end.

"Th-Thank you," Randy managed to stutter. He'd been worried that, as a councilman, Lorian wouldn't like his style—pale green skinny jeans matched with a yellow, short-sleeve button-up. After swallowing hard, Randy murmured, "You look fantastic, too."

The way Lorian's beard graced his lips drew Randy's attention. He couldn't remember the last time he'd kissed someone with facial hair, and he wondered what it would feel like against his own lips. As he stared, they curved into a wider grin.

"Oh, Randy," Lorian crooned, sliding his hands up to cradle his neck. "I had intended to be a gentleman, to wait until after the date, but I cannot resist."

Randy didn't have to wonder long as to what Lorian meant. The larger man dipped his head and sealed his lips over Randy's own. He teased his tongue along Randy's lower lip before nipping gently.

Feeling the hairs slide against his lips, the wet glide of the man's tongue, Randy opened on a gasp. He was in no way virginal, but as he welcomed Lorian's tongue into his mouth and the other man's masculine flavor exploded across his taste buds, every other kiss flew from his mind. Moaning quietly as he met Lorian's questing tongue with his own, Randy searched for more of the other man's flavor.

Lorian met Randy's ardor by feeding him a growl. He slid one hand around to cup his nape, using the move to tilt his head to a better angle. His other hand slid down, down . . .

At first, Randy thought Lorian would grab his butt and haul him close. He seemed to change his mind at the last second. Instead, he slid his arm around his waist, holding him steady as he ravaged Randy's mouth.

Randy gripped Lorian's waist, twisting his fingers in the fabric of his polo shirt, and hung on for the ride.

By the time Lorian broke the kiss, Randy's lungs were screaming for air. He panted harshly as Lorian tucked his face against Randy's neck. Gasping, Randy tipped his head a bit to the side, his head swimming as his body thrummed with fiery need.

"Oh, fucking hell, Randy," Lorian growled against the skin of his neck. "You react so beautifully, my mate. So delicious and responsive."

Lorian tightened his grip on him for a few seconds, continuing to breathe noisily against Randy's neck. The soft beard hairs teased at his skin, sending tingles down Randy's spine. The heady scent of his mate filled his lungs, and his mouth watered for another taste. His nipples beaded, and his cock throbbed.

"Damn it," Lorian growled softly, suddenly easing his hold.

Lorian gripped Randy's shoulders and forced a couple of steps between them. He peered down at him with a strained look on his face.

At first, Randy thought Lorian was rejecting him, and concern flooded him. Then he spotted the heat and need burning within the depths of his dark eyes.

"If we don't stop now, we won't be stopping," Lorian stated gruffly. "And I promised you time."

Randy was so damn tempted to say, *to hell with time*, but he hesitated too long.

Lorian inhaled a slow deep breath, his wide torso expanding and contracting with the move. After that, he released Randy's neck while easing closer. He tightened his arm around Randy's waist and used the hold to start him moving.

"Let's go to lunch," Lorian urged.

Realizing that was probably the wisest action, even if his hard cock didn't think so, Randy nodded.

Chapter Five

Lorian couldn't remember the last time his dick throbbed so badly.

Nearly three hundred years old and I feel like a randy teenager. Randy. Ha! Oh, that's so bad, old man.

Lorian barely resisted rolling his eyes at his arousal-riddled inner dialogue.

With Randy tucked against him as he guided his sweet mate out of the house, he continued to scent him. Unfortunately, that didn't help him.

To Lorian's relief, when he walked outside, the fresh air helped. He opened the back door and assisted Randy into his vehicle. After climbing in beside him, Lorian adjusted his prick, smiling wryly as Randy did the same.

"So, um—" Randy glanced around the interior. "Is Dane and Dakota not coming?"

Lorian pointed toward the front of the limo-style SUV and the closed partition. "Dane is driving. Dakota is up there, too." Lowering his hand on Randy's leg, he squeezed the lean thigh beneath his palm. "Don't worry, my mate. We'll be protected. Councilman Regales Colearian and his mate, Theo, are meeting us there, and they'll have their own guards, too." With a smile, Lorian added, "They'll all sit together at a separate table."

"Okay."

When Lorian scented Randy's unease, it helped to get his arousal in check damn fast. "Randy." Placing his arm around the back of the seat cushion, he half-turned to face his mate.

"Will you share what's bothering you?"

To Lorian's relief, Randy turned and met his gaze. "Why did you decide to change it to a double date?"

That hadn't been what Lorian would have thought Randy would ask. It was a relief, actually. He'd feared Randy already felt overwhelmed with the need for discreet security.

Answering honestly, Lorian told him, "For two reasons. First, as much as I want you all to myself, I thought an outing with others would be a more relaxed feel for our first date." Winking, he stated, "After all, I'm having a hard time keeping my hands to myself." Lorian sobered as he continued, "Also, I know you'll face opposition from a few people, my mother included. I wanted you to meet people who would be supportive. People other than enforcers. Most of the councilmembers won't say one word against it, and the single one that will is once again under review."

"You mean Councilman Peregrine," Randy murmured, proving that he'd heard at least some things from Germaine.

"Exactly," Lorian confirmed. "I want you to know that there are plenty of people who'll be very happy for us."

Randy blew out a breath through pursed lips even as he nodded. "Um, what if they don't like me?" Slapping a hand over his forehead, he groaned. "I'm sorry. I didn't used to be this insecure."

Lorian lowered the arm that was across the back of the seat, draping it over Randy's shoulders. Tugging his mate to him, he tucked him close to his side. Then Lorian dipped his head and nuzzled his mate's temple.

"I know fitting our lives together is going to take some work," Lorian began slowly. "But whether or not friends or family like you will never deter me from being with you." Realizing that left room for question—as if there *were* reasons he wouldn't want to be with Randy—Lorian quickly amended, "There is *nothing* in this world that would make me not want to be with you." Lifting his left hand, he gently touched Randy's cheek. "You're my gift from the gods."

Randy nuzzled into his fingers, his eyelids sliding closed. "You must think I'm such a dumb, inexperienced kid," he murmured, not meeting his gaze. Scoffing softly, Randy continued, "Nothing is further from the truth, actually, but I didn't know fated mates existed until last month. This is"—Randy opened his eyes and met Lorian's gaze—"This feels like fantasy to me. Like it's all too easy."

Nodding, Lorian understood perfectly. "Like the other shoe is going to drop at any moment," he murmured as he swept his gaze over Randy's beautiful features. "Like the floor is going to drop out from under you."

"Yes," Randy whispered, his expression earnest.

Unable to help himself, Lorian pressed his lips to Randy's. His mate was just too damn alluring. He kept it light, just a chaste peck, even though he would have loved to have deepened it and tasted Randy fully once more.

Except, Lorian knew if he did that, he wouldn't be able to pull back a second time. His buffalo already rode him hard, demanding they claim their other half. He'd had a difficult night, wrestling with his beast, who'd wanted to return to Germaine's and whisk his mate home with him.

Lorian lifted his head and smiled down at Randy. He loved the wet sheen on his kiss-swollen lips as well as the dilation of his pretty hazel eyes. Smug satisfaction filled Lorian that he had put that expression on his face.

"Your kisses scramble my brain," Randy murmured, staring at him with wonder. "Never felt anything like it."

Chuckling, Lorian straightened in his seat, although he didn't remove his arm. "Everything between mates is heightened," he reminded Randy, waggling his eyebrows. "Everything."

"Including getting hurt if something goes wrong."

Lorian bit back a sigh upon hearing Randy's whispered comment. He would bet his bottom dollar that his pretty mate hadn't meant to say that out loud. Knowing from where it stemmed—Randy's long-time partner had walked away after meeting his fated mate—Lorian wished he could kick Cranston's ass himself.

Huh. Maybe I will at that.

After all, Lorian knew Cranston had been the one to tweak reports making the alphas of those northern packs believe that Fate did not pair those of the same sex.

"No pain," Lorian decided to comment before placing another kiss to Randy's temple. When he lifted his head, he spotted the blush on Randy's cheeks. "We'll get through this, my mate." Deciding it was time for a subject change, Lorian told him, "We're going to a local crab shack known for their seafood. You're from Massachusetts, right? I was hoping you'd like it."

Just as Lorian had hoped, Randy's countenance brightened. "Yes, that's right." He smiled. "I love seafood. What's this place's specialty?"

Lorian hummed as he thought about the options there. "Well, just about everything they make is fantastic," he told him. "They have a crab salad that's killer, but many people swear by the crawfish bucket."

A smile curved Randy's lips, and his scent of happiness filled the cab.

Even more delicious than the crab.

Feeling the car slow, Lorian looked out the window. He spotted the restaurant a block down the road. The quaint, small-town feel of this end of town always surprised him, especially considering how busy the streets became just ten minutes away.

"Oh, wow," Randy murmured, looking left and right. "This has a wonderful, small-town feel to it." He focused on Lorian. "Are we very far from the city?"

"Not far at all," Lorian revealed as the vehicle came to a stop. He gripped Randy's hand when he reached for the handle, squeezing lightly. "Downtown is less than a half an hour away. This place is a tourists' gem."

"Definitely!" Randy glanced at where Lorian held his wrist, then glanced outside, probably noticing how Dakota and Dane were surveying the area. "Oh."

Lorian smiled and shrugged. "You'll get used to it."

I hope.

To Lorian's relief, Randy nodded.

After Dane opened the door, Lorian exited first. He held out his hand, offering it to Randy. His mate took it easily, but to his surprise, after exiting, Randy made an attempt to release him.

Lorian tightened his hold as he started them down the sidewalk toward the café. "Is this not okay?" he asked curiously, squeezing Randy's fingers in emphasis. "I like touching you."

"I like touching you, too," Randy replied softly. "I just didn't want to presume."

"What do you mean?"

Lorian could guess at what Randy meant, but he wanted his mate to confide in him.

"I mean, you're this powerful councilman," Randy began slowly. Using his free hand, he indicated himself. "And I'm just some guy from a small town. I didn't want to assume that you would want everyone to peg us as a couple at first glance."

Yup. That's what I thought he was worried about.

Spotting a pair of women coming out of the store ten feet in front of them, Lorian called, "Good afternoon, ladies."

They smiled and murmured *good afternoons* back.

Lorian released Randy's hand only to wrap his arm around his mate's waist. "This is the man I plan to marry soon. Isn't he a looker?"

The women laughed and nodded.

"He's a cutie," one stated.

The other grinned and offered, "Congratulations."

Then the pair passed them with a wave, continuing on their way.

Lorian squeezed Randy's waist and started them moving again. "I will never deny you," he vowed. He didn't wait for Randy to reply. Looking forward, Lorian spotted their dining companions. "There's Regales." He pointed at a bearded man with nape-length black hair with touches of gray. He had his arm around a muscular, blue-eyed man. "And his partner, Theo." Lorian purposefully watched his language, hoping Randy caught on.

"Do I need to use a title or call him sir?" Randy asked softly, having obviously noticed.

Shaking his head, Lorian replied, "Not unless we're at headquarters and in a meeting." He truly doubted that would ever happen.

Randy nodded.

"Regales," Lorian called, grinning. "Thanks for meeting us here."

Turning toward them, Regales smiled widely. "I'll never say no to crab legs."

Lorian laughed, knowing how true that was. The grizzly shifter loved seafood of all kinds.

Dipping his chin in Randy's direction, Lorian stated, "This is Randy Cullers, my new partner." He'd already told Regales that he'd met his fated mate, so he would bet Theo knew, too.

"Congratulations," Regales stated with a smile, holding out his hand. "Nice to meet you."

After Randy shook the councilman's hand, Theo grinned broadly and offered his mate a fist-bump. "Congrats, man." He winked as he added, "Guess your man's pretty fine." Then Theo smirked up at his large shifter lover. "Though he don't hold a candle to mine."

Randy snorted and shook his head, and Lorian appreciated Theo's attempt at levity. He glanced around and noticed Enforcer Austin and Enforcer Laudlin standing nearby chatting with Dane and Dakota.

Lorian exchanged a quick nod with the pair, acknowledging them, before focusing back on Regales. "Ready to head in?"

"Already put our name on the list," Regales told them. "We should be seated any time—"

"Theo, party of four?"

"There we are," Theo stated with a grin. As they headed toward the front door, he added, "Reggie likes to use my name, since it's easier for people to pronounce." Seeing Regales frown at Theo, Lorian watched the human laugh as he added, "He also doesn't like to be called Reggie."

"I know you only do it to tease," Regales grumbled.

Theo sobered, bumping into his lover. "So you know I appreciate you."

When Regales smiled down at Theo, the love in his eyes was on clear display.

I want that. Lorian focused on Randy and smiled, liking how his mate smiled back. *We'll get there.*

"Good afternoon, gentlemen," the hostess greeted. "Would you like a table inside or on the deck?"

Lorian focused on Randy, and he didn't miss how everyone else did, too.

Randy's eyes widened as he glanced between them. "U-Um. Wh-What do you think?"

"Seeing as it's your first time here, let's check out the deck." Theo threw him a bone. "It's a gorgeous day, and the view is pretty nice, too." With a wink, he added, "And I don't mean our partners."

Snickering, Randy glanced between Lorian and Regales. "Although, it doesn't hurt, huh?"

Theo grinned broadly. "It surely does not."

"Right this way, please, gentlemen," the hostess urged, mirth filling her tone.

The group followed, and Lorian couldn't resist resting his hand possessively on Randy's back. He felt the way his mate instinctively pressed into his touch, and a smile of satisfaction curved his lips. Even knowing it was a subconscious thing, it still pleased him.

They walked through the restaurant to a door off to the side. After climbing a set of stairs, a deck spread before them. It contained eight tables, each with a fantastic view of the ocean in the distance.

"Oh, wow," Randy murmured appreciatively, pausing to stare. "Good call, Theo."

Theo patted Randy on the shoulder as he passed him. "If it's a windy day, eating up here sucks, but today is about perfect."

Randy chuckled and started moving again, so Lorian followed. Once they'd taken seats at a round table, he shifted his seat closer to Randy. When his mate flashed a smile his way, Lorian winked, rested his arm on the back of his mate's chair, and proceeded to share his sweet fox's menu.

It was all an excuse to be close because Lorian already knew what he was getting.

"Do you want to share the fried clam strips appetizer?" Theo asked, his focus on his menu.

Lorian peered at Randy and arched one brow in silent question.

Humming, Randy smiled and nodded. "Yes, please."

"Sweet," Theo replied. "Then I think I'll get the dungeness crab steam pot."

"Good afternoon, gentlemen."

A male voice drew Lorian's focus from his study of Randy's face as he read the menu. A blond-haired human stood between Theo and Randy's chairs. He smiled at everyone as he began placing large glasses of water before each of them.

"I'm Todd, and I'll be your waiter today," he told them. "Can I get any of you something other than water? Or maybe an appetizer or two started?"

Regales smiled at their waiter. "I'll have whatever *Hefeweizen* you have on tap," he told him. "And we'll take an order of the crab cakes as well as the fried clam strips."

"Oh, excellent choices, sir," Todd replied. He tucked the platter under his armpit, pulled out a pad of paper, and jotted a few notes. Once he'd lifted his head, he focused on Theo. "And you, sir?"

"I'd like a bottle of *Amberbock*, please, Todd," Theo told him.

Without giving it much thought, Lorian ordered a bottle of white wine to split with Randy. After the waiter had left, he realized he should have double-checked that with his mate. Doing something he hadn't needed to in centuries, he fought back a blush.

"Uh, hope that was okay," Lorian commented, worry filling him.

Randy grinned at him, dispelling his concern. "I was going to order a glass of that. This is even better." Peering at him from beneath his lashes, he murmured, "Thank you. I never would have pegged you as a white wine drinker."

"I'm not just a white wine drinker," Lorian countered, pleasure filling him. "I'm an enthusiast. I can't wait to show you my wine cellar."

When Randy's hazel eyes lit up and he nodded eagerly, Lorian could think only of the fact that it would mean getting his mate within his home.

Hearing Regales and Theo both chuckle pulled Lorian from his erotic thoughts.

Chapter Six

Randy could easily guess at Lorian's thoughts when he spotted the heat in the bigger shifter's eyes. His body heated as arousal began to simmer through his veins. If there hadn't been the absolutely perfect sea breeze, Randy knew he would be sweating in his thin shirt.

Out of the corner of his eye, Randy noticed Dakota and his group being led to a nearby table by the hostess. He smiled at his new friend before turning his attention back to the menu.

"What's calling your name, sweetheart?" Lorian asked softly, making the simple question seem almost like an erotic suggestion.

Randy turned his head to meet Lorian's gaze. He saw the heat in the man's brown depths. If they hadn't been in the middle of a restaurant, he would have leaned forward and captured his full mouth.

Lorian smiled a little as he whispered, "I can be on the dessert menu."

Groaning, Randy turned away. "You're not helping," he mumbled, shifting uncomfortably in his chair.

Feeling Lorian's fingertips brush over his shoulder, Randy refocused on him. "Sorry about that," the buffalo shifter murmured. While his expression appeared chagrined, there was a definite twinkle in his dark eyes. "So . . . I'm getting a mess of oysters as well as cold shrimp cocktails. How about you?"

Randy forced his brain to focus on something other than sex. After all, his stomach was rumbling. If he did give in to his urges, he would need all the stamina he could get.

"I'm having trouble deciding between the steamer clams and the snow crab legs," Randy admitted. Then he spotted something else on the menu that he bet would taste delicious. "Oh, and they have corn on the cob in their steamer buckets."

Lorian grinned broadly and told him, "Get everything." Leaning close, he reminded on a murmur, "We're shifters, sweetheart. I'm sure we can pack it all away."

Randy hesitated an instant, looking at the prices.

Evidently, Lorian figured out what was concerning him, for he rested his free hand over the menu. "Stop looking at the prices, Randy." He leaned close and pecked a kiss to his temple before whispering into his ear, "I'm rich, and I never spend my money on anything, so please . . . let me spoil you."

While Randy's skulk hadn't been poor, by any means, he and Cain had still needed to budget their money. He couldn't imagine being able to go to a restaurant and buying everything he wanted without giving it a second thought. Randy focused on Lorian for a long moment, trying to decide if he could just let go like that.

Lifting his hand, Lorian touched his jaw. "Please."

Finally, Randy nodded. "Okay."

"Thank you." Then Lorian pecked a kiss to his lips. Lifting his head, he appeared extremely pleased. "Ah, here comes the wine."

Randy figured Lorian pointed that out just to change the subject, but he was okay with that. Besides, he was looking forward to trying the wine. He focused in the direction Lorian indicated and spotted Todd carrying a tray laden with their drinks.

"Hello again, gentlemen," Todd greeted with a smile. He placed the beers on the table first before adding the wine glasses and the bottle. After setting the tray on a nearby empty table, Todd pulled an opener from his apron and began opening the wine. As he did that, he glanced between Lorian and Randy. "Which of you gentlemen would like to try the wine?"

Lorian immediately indicated Randy. "Give it a try, Randy," he urged. "Make certain you like it."

After nodding, Randy watched Todd pour a small bit into a glass. He took it and sniffed it, enjoying the scent of the fruity undertones. Then he took a sip. The light notes danced pleasantly across his taste buds, so he took another, larger swallow.

Randy hummed and nodded.

Grinning, Lorian smiled at Todd. "That's a yes."

Todd returned Lorian's smile, which sent a completely irrational stab of jealousy through Randy's gut. He furrowed his brows as he stared at his wine glass. Never once had he ever felt jealousy when someone had smiled like that at Cain.

"Hey." Lorian scraped his fingernails over Randy's neck lightly, sending pleasant chills down his neck. "Will you share what popped into your head?"

Yanking his focus from his refilled stemware, Randy glanced around. Todd was gone. He had no idea when he'd become so lost in thought.

"These mating urges are really weird," Randy whispered, feeling completely out of sorts.

"You got that right," Theo agreed, leaning his forearms on the table and wrapping his hands around his beer. Lowering his voice, he assured, "Once you've completed your bond and have been together for a while, the weird mood swings will ease."

Blowing out a breath, Randy could only hope so. "I got upset because our server smiled at you." He squinted at Lorian. "It was so weird."

Lorian's expression turned to understanding. "I get it," he admitted. "Every time someone looked at your very fine ass in those skinny jeans as we walked to the table, I wanted to gouge their eyes out of their head."

Randy barked a laugh, his anxiety easing. "I didn't notice anyone checking me out." Then, unable to help himself, he quipped, "I was too busy admiring you."

Grinning, Lorian winked. "Good." Then he told him, "I ordered for you. I hope you don't mind." Lorian glanced over his shoulder as if searching for the waiter. "If you want something other than what you mentioned earlier, we'll add it as soon as Todd gets back. He was supposed to be getting our appetizers."

"No, I don't need anything else." Then Randy considered what Lorian had said earlier. "Well, I don't think so."

"Don't worry," Regales cut in. "No one ever walks away hungry from this place." He relaxed back in his own chair, slinging his arm over the back of Theo's. "The food is too good."

Theo nodded just as his eyes lit up, his focus somewhere over Randy's shoulder. "Appetizers are comin'." He hummed with excitement.

Randy chuckled softly at his antics, impressed by how comfortable he was, not only in his own skin, but by how he didn't seem to have any trouble showing those same antics in front of others. He wasn't certain when the last time was that he felt that way. Living in his skulk with Cain, they'd had to be careful. There certainly hadn't been any kisses, to the temple or otherwise.

I can have that here. Randy peered Lorian's way, admiring his gorgeous frame and the easy smile curving his lips. *With him.*

Lorian caught him looking and stared right back at him. He even teased his fingertips along the back of his neck.

"Here are your crab cakes and fried clam strips," Todd stated, cutting into their moment.

Jerk.

"Is there anything else I can get you?" Todd continued.

"Another couple of beers," Regales claimed, indicating his and Theo's nearly empty mugs.

Randy didn't even know when they'd drank them.

Huh.

"We're good," Lorian assured, reaching for one of the small plates as he glanced Randy's way.

Smiling and nodding, Randy murmured his thanks. He turned his attention to the food as he watched Regales place a crab cake on Theo's plate. The big shifter took two for himself. Holding up the plate, Regales offered it to Randy.

Lorian beat him to it. He took the plate and slid a cake onto it. Next, he picked up the clam strip boat, giving him a helping of those, too.

Randy licked his lips, anticipation filling him.

An hour and a half later, Randy groaned softly. He leaned back in his chair and rubbed his stomach. His body ached and not from arousal.

"Why did you let me eat so much," Randy whined, pouting. "I can't remember ever being so stuffed."

Lorian massaged Randy's nape gently. "I'm sorry, sweetheart." His dark eyes held a hint of worry. "Are you okay?"

Realizing he was truly concerning Lorian, Randy smiled up at him. "I'm okay," he assured. Trying to sit up, he winced. "Or I will be." Nibbling his bottom lip, Randy asked, "Can we take a walk, maybe? I really need to stretch."

"That sounds like a fantastic idea," Lorian agreed. He turned his attention to their dining companions and asked, "Care to join us?"

Randy didn't mind a bit when they agreed. While Regales had been quiet, he hadn't been standoffish. He just had a habit of smiling indulgently at Theo while allowing his human to run away with the conversation. Theo had been in the military, had seen many different places, and had some fascinating tales to tell—both funny and scary.

"The marshland preserve walkway is only a two-minute stroll from here," Theo pointed out, rising from his seat. The human seemed to know where everything was. "They have a boardwalk with plaques giving information about the preserve and its animals."

"That sounds interesting," Randy stated, looking Lorian's way hopefully. "Do you have time?"

Lorian wrapped his arm around Randy, saying, "I have all the time in the world, sweetheart."

Randy forced himself to ease forward, ignoring the twinge in his overly full belly.

Quickly rising to his feet, Lorian held out his hand. Both Lorian and Regales had already paid, after arguing about who would cover what. Finally, they'd split the bill amicably, with a bit of ribbing back and forth.

Grabbing Lorian's hand, Randy bit his lip as he rose to his feet. He fought against his urge to stretch his hands over his head. He knew that if he twisted this way and that, he could get his stuffed belly to settle a little.

"Do you need to use the men's room or anything before we go?" Lorian asked.

"I do," Theo answered.

"Group trip to the men's room," Regales stated, a lecherous smile taking over his features.

Theo narrowed his eyes. "Oh, no, big guy." He placed his palm on the larger man's chest and flexed his arm, appearing to be keeping him at bay. "You can use a urinal."

Regales heaved a put-upon sigh, even as his dark eyes twinkled. "Taking away all my fun."

Smirking, Theo started toward the stairs. "The men's room is this way," he told him. "Let's hit it."

"I'll let the guys know where we're going," Regales stated, catching Theo's hand, making him pause. "Then I'll join you."

"Sounds good," Theo replied, tipping his head up, obviously expecting a kiss.

Regales didn't leave him hanging, dipping his head and pecking his lips. After that, Regales released Theo, and the human started on his way again.

Feeling Lorian slip his arm around his waist, Randy began moving, too. He paused at the top of the stairs to take one more look at the view before heading down them. He moved into the building and blinked once, allowing his eyes to adjust to the dimmer lighting after being so long in the sun, even on a sun-shaded patio.

Just as they reached the door to the men's room, Lorian's phone rang. He frowned upon reading the screen—Igor, Randy noticed. "Huh. I better take this."

Randy couldn't help but ask, "Who?"

Lorian dipped his head and kissed Randy's temple before whispering, "One of my enforcers."

Nodding, Randy headed through the door that Theo had disappeared through. He spotted two open urinals and a stall. The stall's door was already closed and locked, so Randy assumed Theo was inside it, recalling how he'd ordered Regales to use a urinal.

Wonder if there's a story there.

Randy smirked as he headed to the urinal, recalling many times when he and Cain had gotten naughty in a club's men's room. As he pulled out his dick so he could empty his bladder, he realized he hadn't felt even a twinge of upset at the memory. Instead, he'd immediately wondered if he could coax Lorian into doing something so . . . controversial, dangerous? He wasn't certain what.

Randy had just tucked himself away and was about to flush when he heard the door behind him open. At first, he would have thought it was one of their men, but the guy's scent wasn't familiar. He wondered what was keeping them as he quickly did up his fly.

As soon as Randy reached the sink, the new arrival shoved him forward. He caught himself on the sides of the pedestal sink so he didn't crack his head into the mirror. Tipping his head up, Randy glared into a smirking, dark-skinned visage.

"I got a message for you, twink," the man stated, his lip curling. "Move on from the councilman or else."

Sucking in a shocked gasp, Randy noticed the scent of feline shifter, although he couldn't pin what kind.

"Or else what?"

The man pivoted.

The move gave Randy enough room to maneuver away from the sink and toward the stall wall.

Scoffing, the large black male curled his lip at Theo. "You're Regales's fuck-toy." He shook his head as he eyed Theo with distaste. "Don't worry. We'll clear out your kind soon enough."

Theo didn't appear even the slightest bit concerned. In fact, he even looked at his fingernails as if he was checking them out of boredom.

"You know," Theo began, his tone dry. "I'm pretty sure that my man and his people are going to want to question you about your rude comments in here."

"They won't ever know about it if you guys aren't here when they come lookin'," the belligerent cat shifter claimed as he took one step toward Theo.

"We'll be here," Theo countered. In the next instant, he pulled something from behind his back, pointed, and fired.

A dart jabbed into the shifter's t-shirt-clad pectoral. The male snarled for an instant. Then the guy's eyes rolled to the back of his head, and he dropped unceremoniously to the floor.

Randy stared at their attacker for a few seconds before focusing on Theo. "I have two questions."

"Only two?" Theo stared at the shifter. "I have plenty more

than that for this guy."

Shrugging, Randy admitted, "I can't help with that. Not my thing." He pointed at Theo as the human arched one brow his way. "Where were you hiding that thing? And how can I get hold of one?"

If Randy was going to run into this often, he wanted to be prepared. He was never one to run from trouble, although he did his best to avoid it. Randy would never leave his mate to fight a battle on his own.

Yep, guess there really is no way I'm leaving my mate. Especially not now. He's mine.

Chapter Seven

"I want to know who the fuck that guy is, and I want to know who sent him."

Lorian seethed, barely managing to keep from roaring the words. His brand new mate had been attacked in a fucking bathroom on their very first date. He didn't even know how anyone had found out about Randy or where they were going.

Who the fuck tipped off some hater?

Knowing every single one of the men at Germaine's barbeque, Lorian couldn't imagine that any of them would. They were all loyal to the council as well as happy for same-sex fated pairings. Hell, most of them were bisexual or gay themselves.

Was it possible that someone had overheard his conversation with Regales? But that would mean it was someone in either of their households. He hated that idea just as much.

"I've already put a call in to my brother," Dane told Lorian, referring to the eldest of the trio, Delanrue. "He's meeting me at headquarters. He'll get to the bottom of this."

Taking a deep breath, Lorian nodded. He knew Delanrue was the best damn interrogator the council had. When several Council Enforcers had defected after a couple of councilmen had gone rogue, joining them, never had he been more grateful that the Drudeson brothers had remained loyal.

"I'm fine," Randy assured, rubbing Lorian's chest. "We're both fine." Then he growled, "And I want one of those dart guns and for Theo to teach me how to use it."

"You do?" Lorian snapped his focus back to his mate, whom he hadn't been able to release as soon as he'd walked into the bathroom and saw the pair standing over the downed man. "Why?"

Randy peered seriously at him. "Well, if I'm going to stand by your side against these jerks, then I need a way to protect myself."

The words clicked around in Lorian's brain for a few heartbeats before they actually registered. Then his breath caught in his throat. "You're going to stay by my side?" Tightening his hold, Lorian couldn't even wait for Randy to respond, hurrying to add, "Anything. Anything to make you more comfortable. I'll see that it's done."

Dane growled softly as he hefted the unconscious shifter over his shoulder. "Is the coast clear, Dakota?"

While it was crowded in the bathroom with the five of them in there, Dakota still didn't look pleased to leave. Still, he eased the door open and stepped out. Then he poked his head back in and told them, "Austin and Laudlin are guarding the opening to the halls. Coast is clear."

Nodding, Dane slipped around Lorian and Randy, taking their attacker with him. As soon as he exited, Dakota joined them again. He glanced between them, frowning.

"No more trips to a restaurant's men's room by yourself," Dakota grumbled, crossing his arms over his chest. "I've been your bodyguard less than twenty-four hours, and already someone has targeted you. What the fuck?"

Lorian wondered the same damn thing.

Randy nodded. "I think I'm going to need to learn more about what's going on." Frowning, he added, "Because he called Theo a fuck-toy, not a mate. Is someone still feeding others lies, or do they really just not believe what's right in front of their noses?"

"A bit of both, probably," Dakota grumbled, leading the

way out of the restroom.

"Where'd Theo and Regales go?" Randy asked, glancing around.

"I think Regales took Theo home to fuck him," Dakota replied bluntly. "Reaffirm their bond, confirm that Theo is alive and healthy, all that shit."

Lorian growled softly, wishing he could do the same damn thing. His buffalo was driving him hard to take Randy home and check him for injuries. It didn't matter that his mate had told him he was fine. Lorian needed to see for himself.

Randy must have read his mind, for he peered at him through his lashes. "Can we take a raincheck on the nature walk?"

"I'll take you back there anytime you wish," Lorian replied, his breath catching at the scent of need that began to flood Randy's scent. "What would you like, my mate?"

Dakota had been guiding them out the back door. Stepping into the alley, he spotted his mini-SUV limo. He guided Randy toward it while waiting with bated breath for his mate's response.

Stopping beside the vehicle, Randy inhaled deeply while gripping Lorian's hands tightly. "I'm ready for you to claim me," he blurted out.

Then Randy's face turned beet red as he glanced Dakota's way. Dane had been replaced by Igor—whom Lorian had already introduced to Randy, so his mate knew who he was—but neither shifter was looking their way. Instead, they were monitoring the area.

Lorian cupped Randy's jaw and urged his focus back to him. "I would love to take you home and claim you, Randy." He paused a second. Knowing he had to ask, he added, "If you're certain, but what changed?"

Randy lifted his chin and met his gaze squarely. "The idea of losing you, of being forced to walk away from you, even after less than twenty-four hours . . . it damn near gutted me." Resting his palms on Lorian's chest, Randy nuzzled his palm. "I'm yours, and you're mine. I understand that now." His smile turned a little sad as he added, "I can admit it now, but Cain was a much stronger man than I could ever be."

While Lorian didn't really have a desire to discuss Randy's ex-partner, he would never ignore something that seemed important to his soon-to-be lover. To that end, he stated, "While I'll never believe that, why do you think so?"

Randy shook his head just a little, not enough to dislodge Lorian's hand. "Because he offered to hold off on pursuing his mate until he came back into the city. That would have been three weeks," he explained, grimacing. "He wanted to make certain I would be okay, and I don't think I could leave you for three weeks . . . even to make sure he was okay to move on."

Having heard the highlights of the tale from Germaine, Lorian confidently claimed, "You were just as strong and courageous but in another way." Seeing Randy's expression turn disbelieving, he told him, "You encouraged him to embrace his future."

Personally, Lorian thought Cain had been willing to hide behind Randy and his need for time when it was really the man's own fear of change. He would never say that out loud, however. Never would Lorian besmirch Randy's memory of his ex.

Lorian planned to lift up Randy's own image of himself, instead. After losing the man, even though he'd encouraged it, his mate's self-esteem had obviously taken a knock. He would always be happy that it had brought Randy to him, however.

"I just wanted him to be happy." Grimacing, Randy admitted, "And I couldn't do that. Not by myself."

Nodding, Lorian understood. "You occasionally needed a

third because he was a switch." Seeing Randy's eyes widen, he quickly murmured, "Germaine didn't want me to find out in some odd way, as if there were secrets, that you used to . . . well, with Sage."

As much as Lorian knew it was in the past—way-too-recent past, but still the past—he still couldn't say it out loud.

"Damn, they really did tell you everything," Randy grumbled, annoyance flooding his scent.

"Not everything," Lorian countered, urging him into the limo. Once they were seated, Randy tucked close in his arms, Lorian stated, "I plan to learn the sounds of your mewls and all the best places to touch you all by myself."

Randy groaned softly, a shudder working through his lithe body. "I'd like the sound of that."

"Then let's get started."

Lorian knew it took a good thirty-five to forty minutes to get from the restaurant to his home. That was more than enough time to play a little with his lover. He had every intention of seeing what kind of noises he could pull from Randy as he sucked his dick.

Sliding from the seat, Lorian pushed Randy's legs wide. He eased between them as he rubbed his palms up his gorgeous mate's green-jeans-covered thighs.

"L-Lorian?" Randy's breathing hitched. "Wh-What?"

Humming appreciatively at the intensifying aroma of arousal, Lorian cupped Randy's crotch with his thumbs and forefingers. He pressed down, accentuating the hard rod trapped behind the fabric of his mate's fly. His mouth watered with his desire to taste him.

"Gonna suck your dick, Randy," Lorian declared as he reached for his zipper. Freezing with the tab between his thumb and forefinger, he met Randy's gaze squarely. "Are you okay with that? It will start the bonding process."

Randy's nostrils flared, and his body trembled beneath Lorian's grip. "I'm more than ready," he declared breathily. He gripped the leather seat on either side of his legs as he spread his thighs even wider. "J-Just never thought y-you'd—" Randy caught his lower lip between his teeth.

Lorian realized Randy did that when he wanted to stop himself from saying something that might upset whoever he was with. He would bet his bottom dollar that he'd started the habit so he didn't annoy his ex. Again, he would never call attention to it in that manner.

Instead, Lorian rose higher on his knees as he carefully began lowering his lover's fly. He kissed Randy, taking his plump flesh between his own. Sucking the abused appendage free, he kissed it gently before releasing it and easing back from Randy.

"My sweetheart," Lorian crooned, doing his best to keep his expression kind. "I wish to hear your thoughts." He eased the flap wide, admiring the long, slender length that pushed from between them. "All of them." Lorian tore his gaze from the weeping prick he intended to suck. "Otherwise, how will we get to know each other?"

Randy stared at him for a heartbeat, two, before whispering, "You're a big dominant top. Never thought you'd be willing to suck dick."

"Not anyone's dick," Lorian countered, taking Randy's rod in his hand. "Just yours." Then Lorian lowered his head and rubbed his bearded cheek from root to tip, all while holding Randy's gaze. "Only yours."

Hearing Randy's moan, seeing the flush on his cheeks and neck, Lorian reveled in the responses. He gripped his mate's hips and urged his lover's pants farther down. It was Lorian's turn to moan.

"You shave."

"D-Do you mind?" Randy's worry filled his tone.

Ever-so-gently, Lorian teased his fingertips over the smooth, hairless skin of Randy's groin. He moaned again, matching the husky whimper of his lover. Unable to help himself, Lorian dipped his head again, rubbing his beard hairs over the smooth flesh.

"Love it," Lorian reassured.

Randy groaned and arched beneath his ministrations, and Lorian used his hold on his forever lover's hips to keep him from moving too far. He licked and sucked the skin all around his mate's erection, teasing and nipping. He became enamored with Randy's mewls, moans, shudders, and twitches.

"You're so perfect," Lorian mumbled against Randy's flesh. "So very perfect."

"L-Lorian," Randy whined. "Pleeeeasssse."

Lorian lifted his head just enough to admire Randy's flushed face and neck. His abdominals fluttered beneath his form-fitting shirt. It was the pre-cum wetting the head of his mate's dick that made his mouth water.

Opening, Lorian wrapped his lips around the crown and suckled. He swept his tongue over the flared head, licking up his mate's juices. The lightly salted fluid burst across his taste buds, making him wish for more.

"Oh, gods!"

Smiling around his tasty mouthful, Lorian sucked harder as he took him deep. He teased his fingertips over Randy's balls as he swallowed around his crown. Then he slowly drew back off, making certain Randy felt every inch.

"I-I-I—"

Lorian had a pretty good idea what Randy was trying to get out, and he couldn't wait. Pressing against the sensitive patch behind Randy's balls, he took his new and forever lover's cock deep again. His ministrations were rewarded.

Randy's body tried to buck, Lorian's hand holding him steady on the seat. He swallowed quickly as his lover's balls pumped a thick stream of seed down his throat. Pulling partway off so the next shot hit his tongue, he rolled the tasty cum across his taste buds. Lorian swallowed that, too, just in time to receive another mouthful.

For several seconds, Lorian relished in the simple action of drinking Randy's seed and petting his abdominals, bringing his mate back from the throes of orgasm. He eased off his fox's softening prick when his grunt hinted at discomfort. Lorian peered at his lover, admiring the bliss-drunk, glazed expression on his face.

Beautiful.

"You're gorgeous in your pleasure," Lorian crooned, slipping his hands under Randy's shirt and running them up his torso. "Absolutely stunning." When his lover met his gaze, blinking blearily, Lorian purred, "I plan to put that expression on your face often."

"Yes, please."

Lorian chuckled huskily as he leaned forward. Resting his hands on the seat to either side of Randy's thighs, he brought their faces close. He saw the happy and relaxed gleam in his lover's eyes right before he sealed his lips over the other shifter's.

Randy immediately opened to him, and Lorian took complete advantage. He delved his tongue deep, allowing his mate to taste himself on his tongue. His lover's flavor of seafood, wine, and something all his own set his taste buds on fire anew.

Groaning softly, Lorian pulled away gently. His throbbing cock warned him that if he didn't get some control, he would be shooting in his pants like an untried youth. As good as that sounded, Lorian didn't want that to be his first time with his mate, either. He had every intention of shooting either in Randy's mouth or his ass.

Except, the dual knock on the window separating them from the front told Lorian he didn't have that kind of time.

"Let's get you situated," Lorian urged, gripping Randy's jeans. "We're almost there."

Randy allowed Lorian to help him back into his jeans, even as he began to nibble his bottom lip.

Lorian waited to ask until he'd zipped up his lover's fly. After settling back on the seat, he pulled Randy into his arms. He rubbed up and down his mate's opposite arm while cradling his jaw with the other.

"Will you tell me what's on your mind?" Lorian asked, using his thumb to pull Randy's lip away from his teeth.

I like his scent of satisfaction so much better than uncertainty. We don't know each other. We'll get there.

Randy glanced down at Lorian's fly and the obvious bulge behind it. His jeans weren't designed to hide an erection as large as the one Lorian sported. True to his shifter breed, he was hung like a, well, a buffalo, and it showed.

"Um, what about you?" Randy rested his hand on Lorian's thigh . . . really high on his thigh. "I'd love to—"

Lorian groaned and gripped Randy's hand, keeping it from moving and cutting off his words at the same time. "I want that," he assured, not wanting his mate to think he was denying him. "I want that oh-so-badly, but we don't have time." Tipping his chin toward the left window, Lorian told Randy, "We're pulling through my estate's gate." He waggled his brows as he added, "I'll give you a short tour, and we'll see what happens wherever we end up."

Somewhere with lube, to be sure.

Randy stared into his eyes for a second, perhaps searching for reassurance. Finally, he must have found it, for he smiled and nodded. "Sounds good."

Good indeed.

CHAPTER EIGHT

"You live here?" Randy stared in wonder at the beautifully landscaped lawns and the large manor-style home. "It's beautiful."

Randy couldn't even guess at how many landscapers and gardeners would be needed to keep up on such an expansive space.

Lorian hummed, releasing his hold a little, allowing Randy to lean forward and look out the windows. "It is my home. I told you one of my herd-mates was good with computers." After clearing his throat in discomfort, Lorian admitted, "I made certain all my herd-members were set up to their hearts' content while I was alpha. I'm sorry to say that not all of them knew how to keep it."

Grimacing, Randy nodded. "Yeah, sometimes it's not good to have things handed to you like that. If you don't earn it yourself, didn't have to work hard for it"—Randy recalled working plenty of extra hours to buy the perfect sofa for his and Cain's home one Christmas season—"some people have a tendency to squander it. Then they're right back where they started."

Lorian nodded. "Exactly." He pointed toward the left. "There's a four-car garage past the portico, as well as a stable. Do you ride horses?"

Randy's brows shot up as excitement filled him. "I do! I always wanted one, too, but—" He cut himself off, then realized he needed to start sharing with the man who would be his forever love. "Well, Cain didn't like them."

"Ah, well, I love them," Lorian revealed with a wink. "Just another thing that Fate got right." He pecked a quick kiss to his lips, then changed the subject, accepting without making a big deal out of it. "There's also an indoor-outdoor pool in the back with a waterfall and grotto. I had a passage installed that leads directly to it from my en suite bathroom."

Grinning broadly, Randy teased, "You installed a secret passage?"

Lorian laughed as the car came to a stop under the tall stone portico. "It is discreet, so some would call it a secret."

"Any other secret passages?"

Randy's heart raced with the idea of old-world secret passages in his home.

Not that he's asked me to move in yet, or anything.

The door opened as Lorian chuckled softly. He eased out, then offered his hand to Randy, helping him once more. Tucking Randy's hand into the crook of his arm, he waggled his eyebrows playfully.

"There may be one here and there," Lorian told him. "Are you going to squirrel them out?"

Randy nudged into Lorian as he quipped back, "Well, foxes are curious creatures, ya know." Then he sobered and added, "As long as I wouldn't be intruding or something."

Lorian paused at the top of the stone steps even as a black man dressed in black slacks and a pale-blue, short-sleeved button-down held the door open for them. Ignoring the male, Lorian cradled Randy's jaw and eyed him with a serious gaze. "Randy, my home is your home." His dark eyes held a warmth as he added, "You may go anywhere in there that you want, unless it's one of our people's private rooms."

Swallowing hard, Randy nodded. That totally sounded like a proposal to move in to him. He'd watched as Sage had completely uprooted his life after knowing Germaine for just a few hours, and he finally understood why his buddy had done it. Randy wanted to do the same.

And this is the first step.

Realizing Lorian was waiting for some response, Randy smiled up at him and told him, "I can't wait"—taking a chance, he added—"my mate."

The beaming grin Lorian bestowed upon him was more than worth sucking up his courage to say the words out loud.

Lorian once again dipped his head, this time pressing a hard, closed-mouth kiss to his lips. Then he lifted his head and started them into the house. As they passed the ebony-skinned male, Lorian indicated him.

"This is Madison Drossen, an alligator shifter and my butler." Lorian smiled at the male. "He keeps the house running smoothly, so if you need anything, he's the man to see."

"Nice to meet you, Randy," Madison rumbled in a deep bass voice. "Congratulations on finding each other." A wistful gleam entered his dark eyes as he added, "Someday, I hope to be so lucky."

"Then you need to leave the house sometimes, Mads," Lorian teased, patting his shoulder.

Madison rolled his eyes, completely breaking his uptight persona. "I have Thursdays off."

"Then come out with us Wednesday night," Dakota ordered, stopping beside them in the foyer. He grinned broadly. "We'll hit a few bars and have some fun."

Madison hesitated, clearly torn.

"Don't make me order you to go," Lorian threatened, although his tone held a clear note of teasing.

Huffing a deep sigh, Madison grumbled, "Very well."

Dakota laughed, heading into the house.

Turning back to Randy, Madison offered his hand. "Welcome to the household."

Randy took Madison's hand. "Thank you." After the man released him, he finally took a good look around . . . and gaped. "Oh, wow."

Just as one would expect from the look of the outside, the

inside appeared just as magnificent. There was a grand sweeping staircase to the left leading to a balcony and a crystal chandelier overhead. The tile appeared to be marble, extending through the hallway beyond. An open door to the right showcased nice furniture and a fireplace, giving it the look of a sitting room.

"I'll show you the downstairs first," Lorian began, urging Randy toward the hallway. "The right upstairs wing is all suites for those who live and work here," he told him, pointing up in that direction. "The hall to the left leads to my"—he paused a heartbeat, meeting Randy's gaze with an earnest expression as he amended—"*our* rooms. My study is up there as well as a personal library, the master suite and bathroom, and a couple of rooms I don't use much. You'd be welcome to do something with them. I don't know if you have hobbies or anything." Lorian's brows furrowed as he added, "Other than the occasional horseback ride, I'm afraid I'm pretty boring."

Randy smiled up at Lorian, squeezing his arm where it was still tucked in his elbow. "I'm a homebody. As long as there's an awesome fireplace to curl up in front of and read a book, I'll be happy." Knowing he had to be honest, Randy admitted, "Um, I might want to set up a sewing room."

"A sewing room?" Lorian seemed surprised, but not put off by Randy doing something most would consider a female hobby.

Nodding, Randy told him, "Living in Massachusetts near the coast, the winters are cold. I started sewing blankets for warmth and fell in love with the design aspect of it." He couldn't help but smile as he told him, "I branched out into pillows and stuffed animals, and I even started selling them online for extra money."

Lorian grinned at him. "My own little creative entrepreneur." He pecked a kiss to his temple before telling him, "We'll definitely get something set up for you. Just let me know what you need."

Randy nodded, pleasure filling him at Lorian's supportive response.

"This hall on the right leads to guest suites," Lorian pointed to a hall on the right. Pointing left, he told him, "That leads to the ballroom, the main library, an office I use to meet others, if need be, plus a relaxing recreation room as well as the security offices. Beyond all that is the pool."

Before them, Madison opened a set of double doors, revealing a large formal dining room, also done in tasteful opulence.

"Formal dining, obviously," Lorian said with a wink, stopping just inside the doors. He pointed to double swinging doors on the right. "The kitchens." After Madison had opened another set of French doors at the back, Lorian said, "An informal dining. There's back stairs to it, and I'll show you those later." Lorian headed to the final set of French doors to the left. "As I said"—he opened them—"the ballroom."

Randy peered around in awe.

Yep. A ballroom.

The space appeared huge with hardwood floors, a grand piano in the far-right corner, and a stage in the opposite corner to the right. There were a few padded chairs scattered around, which would allow people to rest between dances . . . or cluster and gossip. A bar was built into a corner to the left.

"Do you host balls often?" Randy asked softly, suddenly feeling inadequate. "Because I don't know how to dance." Blushing, he added while flapping his hand at the room. "Well, not *this* kind of dancing."

"Fortunately, not too often," Lorian told him with a smile. "Don't worry"—he winked—"I'll teach you ballroom. It's really not hard as long as you can learn to relax."

"Yeah," Randy grumbled. "Relax in a room full of powerful and rich shifters. Like that'll be easy."

Lorian led him toward a door on the left, returning him to a hallway. "Actually, the balls are normally put on by my mother and host high-ranking and affluent humans." He smirked as he looked down at Randy. "I wonder if she'll carry on that tradition once she realizes I'm not going to mate with someone of her choosing."

"Her choosing?" Latching onto that, Randy wondered, "What's that mean?"

Grimacing, Lorian admitted, "She's always tried to set me up here and there over the centuries, but ever since councilmen have begun finding their mates in males, she's really stepped up her attempts." Cocking his head, Lorian appeared to be thinking hard for a few seconds before telling him, "At least two a month so far, and I know she'd planned to introduce me to someone last night, but I bailed on her gathering."

Randy growled softly, frowning at Lorian. "You're mine," he declared, tightening his grip on his arm. "If some hussy tries to steal you, I'll scratch their eyes out!"

Lorian stared at him with wide eyes.

Realizing what he'd just done, Randy gasped and clapped his free hand over his mouth, shock filling him.

Then Lorian's lips split into a wide, broad grin. His dark eyes twinkled. Turning Randy, he started them walking again.

"Yes, I am," Lorian agreed, pleasure flooding his tone and scent. "I am most definitely yours."

Lorian's next question surprised Randy anew.

"Are you going to claim me?"

Randy froze, then stumbled forward again, since Lorian obviously hadn't been ready for that. He paused and leveled a questioning look his way.

"B-But, um." Randy almost started nibbling his lip but stopped himself just in time. Instead, he blurted out, "But you know I'm a bottom. I don't want to—" Randy waved his hand as if that could finish the sentence for him.

Lorian's expression softened, and he smiled. After pulling

free of Randy's hand, he wrapped both arms around his waist. He tugged him close, flushing their torsos.

Randy tipped his head back a bit so he could meet Lorian's gaze, considering their four-inch height difference.

"I know you're a bottom," Lorian began softly, his voice husky. "And I love that." Dipping his head, he nuzzled the crook of Randy's neck, sending tingles down his spine. "I mean" – he nipped Randy's neck where he'd been nuzzling – "will you bite me here?" Lorian lifted his head again to once more meet his gaze. "Claim me . . . with a bite."

"You want me to?" Randy blurted out the question. While he hadn't considered it, now that the idea had been planted in his brain, his fox yipped in his mind with excitement. His animal was more than on board with the idea.

Grinning, Lorian nodded. "More than I could ever say."

Randy grinned back. "Yes, please."

Lorian groaned, rocking his hips. His eyes dilated, and the scent of his arousal flooded the hallway. "Yesss," he hissed. "Want that, too."

Panting, Randy pressed his quickly growing dick against Lorian's thigh, searching for friction. The huge erection digging into his belly caused his ass to clench, and it wasn't in fear. Randy couldn't wait to feel that monster splitting him wide open.

"I'd hoped to have enough self-control to get through most of the tour," Lorian told him gruffly. "But I don't think I can wait much longer."

"I don't wanna wait anymore," Randy admitted. "Twenty-four hours is long enough, right?"

Lorian chuckled gruffly. "Definitely." He grabbed Randy's hand and tugged. "Come on. Through the pool room is the quickest, at this point."

Randy nodded and followed without resistance. As they hurried down the hall, he glanced left and right. He spotted the huge recreation room and couldn't wait to explore. Same with the library. The doors on the left were closed, so Randy guessed they were the office and security.

Finally, Lorian reached the end of the hall and took him through a clear door with a special seal—probably to make certain the moisture from the pool room didn't get into the rest of the house.

As Randy passed through the huge, glass-encased structure, he gaped. The pool had to be at least a hundred by fifty. There were three levels of diving boards at the deep end. The shallow end had been made up to be a tropical paradise. There was a rock wall with a waterfall and places to sit, recline, and relax.

Lorian crossed to a panel to the left of a glass-fronted cabinet containing two shelves of towels and another two of cushions for the lounge chairs surrounding the pool. He pressed a knot in the wood of the cabinet, causing it to swing open without a sound. There was a spiral staircase within the hidden space.

"Oh, wow," Randy murmured, impressed.

Glancing over his shoulder, Lorian winked at him. Then he began leading him inside.

Randy squeezed Lorian's hand and tugged, regaining his attention. His big mate pinned him with a questioning look.

Pointing back at the waterfall, Randy asked shyly, "Can we, um"—he felt his cheeks heat, but he forced the words out anyway—"claim each other there?" When Lorian followed Randy's gaze and looked indecisive, he added, "I think it'd be super romantic."

Lorian returned his focus to Randy and smiled. "It would be romantic," he agreed softly, stepping backward again. "I'd love to."

Then Lorian swung the door cabinet closed, hiding the stairway. He opened the cabinet's glass doors and slid his hand under the right-most towel on the top shelf. Pulling his hand out again, Lorian held something in his hand.

When Lorian started them toward the pool, Randy realized what it was.

Lube.

Jealousy roared through him. "You fuck people in here often?" he asked, anger filling him.

To Randy's surprise, Lorian grinned widely even as he shook his head. "Nope. Never have before." He held up the lube and revealed, "One of my guards, a vampire enforcer named Jacob, is a horndog"—shrugging, he added—"for obvious reasons."

Right. A vampire needs blood.

"I hear the best way to get blood is through sex," Randy whispered, feeling regret that he'd questioned his mate. "Sorry."

Lorian stopped at the edge of the pool and drew him into his arms once more. Smiling down at him, he revealed, "I love that you get all possessive on me. *Love it.*" Lowering his head, Lorian whispered into his ear, "Never change that."

Then Lorian sealed his lips over Randy's, taking him in a ravishing kiss.

Getting lost in the taste of his lover, Randy decided that he could definitely do that.

Chapter Nine

Lorian loved each and every time Randy showed his possessiveness of him. It meant he was coming to care for him, perhaps even beyond what his natural shifter instincts would create. He hoped so, anyway.

Then Lorian lost himself for several minutes in exploring his lover's mouth. He reveled in the taste of his fox shifter, and he relished the way he responded to his touch. The moans and whimpers Randy fed him were music to Lorian's ears.

When Lorian could no longer ignore his throbbing cock—he couldn't remember the last time he'd been so hard for so long—he broke the kiss. Smug satisfaction flooded him upon seeing Randy's kiss-swollen lips and flushed features. The heady scent of his mate's arousal perfumed the air, beating out the smells of chlorine and cleaner.

"Gonna strip you, sweetheart," Lorian stated, declaring his intention. At the same time, he began doing just that. "Lift your arms."

Lorian gripped the hem of Randy's shirt. After easing it over his lover's head, he dropped it onto a recliner. He reached for the fly of his green jeans next, pausing just long enough to watch Randy toe out of his sandals and kick them aside. For some reason, Lorian even thought his lover's green-painted toes were sexy.

Odd thought.

Dismissing it, Lorian opened Randy's fly, revealing his beautiful erection and his shaved groin, which he was quickly becoming obsessed with. He lowered to one knee, taking

Randy's jeans with him. A second later, Lorian moved one hand to his mate's hip, offering him support as he stepped out of them.

"You're absolutely stunning," Lorian rumbled, sliding his hands up Randy's legs to his hips, then up around his torso. His mate's naturally lighter skin under his tanned hands enticed him to touch him all over. "So beautiful."

Lorian tweaked Randy's nipples between his fingers, tugging a hiss from his mate's lips while causing his erection to twitch. Growling, Lorian did it again and was rewarded with a drop of pre-cum from Randy's slit. He leaned forward and licked it clean before rising to his feet. Otherwise, Lorian knew he would become distracted, and he needed in his mate's ass too badly.

Releasing Randy, Lorian reached for the hem of his shirt. He quickly yanked it over his head and dropped it to the chair. When he could see again, Lorian nearly swallowed his tongue. Randy knelt on one knee, peering at him from beneath his lashes.

"Randy," Lorian groaned, his erection throbbing behind his fly. "Later."

Randy grinned up at him impishly. "Oh, I intend to suck your cock . . . a *lot*," he told him. Then he bent further and touched his shoe-clad foot. "But I have other plans at the moment."

Lorian growled, not at all upset that he'd misunderstood. Resting his hands on Randy's shoulders, he lifted first one foot, then the other, allowing his lover to remove his footwear and socks. When Randy reached for his fly, Lorian swallowed hard, his breath stuttering in his chest. As his mate carefully lowered his zipper, even dipping his slender fingers into the fly to protect his aching shaft, breathing became difficult. His erection twitched in Randy's too-loose hold, and he groaned in a mixture of need and pain.

"Don't worry," Randy assured, his voice breathless. "I'll take ever-so-good care of this."

Then Lorian's little minx gave his erection a squeeze before releasing him in favor of helping him from his jeans.

Growling, Lorian narrowed his eyes as he watched Randy intensely. He noticed the way his mate kept glancing at his cock as he helped first one leg, then the other, from his jeans. To Lorian's relief, there was definite desire and longing, even hunger, on his face and in his eyes, rather than concern or fear.

Lorian knew he was very well-endowed, although he'd never measured.

Waiting only long enough for Randy to rise to his feet, Lorian grabbed his mate around the waist. He continued to hold the lube as he propelled them both into the water. Twisting, Lorian made certain he landed first, feeling the water slap against his back as he kept his lover held securely to his chest.

Straightening in the water, which was only three and a half feet deep, Lorian didn't bother releasing Randy. He wrapped his arm around his mate's bare ass, grabbing the opposite cheek. Wrapping his other arm around Randy's torso, Lorian began wading through the water.

To Lorian's pleasure, Randy wrapped his arms and legs around him, clinging to him as if it was the most natural thing in the world.

Lorian nibbled on Randy's neck as he moved, his focus on the stone seating created near the waterfall. Mentally, he weighed the pros and cons of each one before deciding on a seat that left them up to their chests in water. Lorian sat back, the mist of the waterfall's spray teasing over the left side of his body, but not heavy enough to impede their vision.

As if it was as natural as could be, Randy straddled Lorian's lap, his butt pressed against his thighs and their wet erections pressed firmly together.

Groaning, Lorian couldn't help but buck a little, rutting

against the smaller man in his arms.

Exquisite.

"Wait, wait," Randy gasped, shuddering against him. "Hold on."

Randy's fingernails dug into Lorian's shoulder blades, helping him regain control just a smidge.

Blowing out a breath, Lorian met Randy's gaze. "What is it, sweetheart?" Still, he couldn't keep the growl of need out of his voice.

"Don't want to come like this," Randy declared, his hazel eyes blazing with lust. "I need you in my ass so damn badly."

Lorian moaned roughly. Nodding, he managed to release Randy long enough to lift the lubricant out of the water. He read the label, not at all surprised to find that it was waterproof.

While Lorian had never stumbled upon Jacob fucking in the pool, he'd heard the rumors. That was one of the reasons his cleaners took extra care of the place. It always smelled of bleach, chlorine, and lavender.

"Lift up a little," Lorian urged, pouring a generous dollop onto his fingers before setting the tube on a nearby rock. "I'll try to hurry." Seeing Randy's eager nod as he knelt over him, Lorian admitted, "I need you just as badly, my mate."

Then Lorian skimmed his clean fingers down Randy's ass, found his star, and pushed one lubed digit in as deeply as possible.

"Yessss," Randy hissed, arching his back and pressing back into his ministrations. "Another."

"Pushy bottom," Lorian teased with a light smack to his ass. Still, he did as Randy had bid.

Randy sighed and grinned at him. "I'll ride your cock so good, Lorian." Hunger flooded his expression as he stared down at his prick. "Hurry. I promise you'll love it."

"I know I will."

Lorian figured they'd have plenty of time to learn about

each other after they'd bonded, after their hormones and instincts weren't driving them to couple, to bond.

"I'll give you what you want this time," Lorian told him, easing his two fingers out, then in, out again, then pushing three into his moaning, gorgeous lover. With his fingers in deep, Lorian teased over Randy's prostate, massaging and stimulating his nub. "But know that I'll make you wait next time."

Chuckling, Randy purred, "I can't wait to see you try."

Realizing he had a power bottom on his hands, Lorian laughed darkly. "Challenge accepted."

Then Lorian pulled his fingers free of Randy's body. He grabbed the lube and poured more in his palm before setting it aside again. Reaching beneath the water, Lorian grabbed himself, slicking his dick.

Lorian rested his hands on Randy's hips, met his lover's needy gaze, and ordered, "Ride me, my mate."

Randy's nostrils flared. Somehow, his eyes dilated just a little bit more, the green in his hazel eyes dominating the brown. He nodded, eagerness in the move, before lowering himself deeper into the water.

When Randy's ass bumped his cock head, Lorian gritted his teeth. He released his mate's hip and grabbed his base, steadying his erection. Randy immediately took advantage, pressing down, and in the next instant, Lorian felt his crown encased in the tightest, hottest chute he'd ever experienced.

"Oh, gods," Randy gasped, stilling.

Yanking his attention from where he stared at how he pierced Randy, Lorian saw the way his mate's eyes were heavy-lidded and how he panted harshly.

"Shit," Lorian whispered. "Am I hurting you?" He tightened his hold on Randy's waist and lifted, intending to pull him off. "I should have stretched you more."

It had been centuries since he'd pleasured a male.

Obviously, I'm out of practice and didn't give my mate enough prep.

Disgust at his actions flooded Lorian, easing some of his ardor.

"No, stop. Stop," Randy demanded, resisting him. "Just give me a sec."

Lorian met Randy's gaze and waited, swallowing hard. "Randy?" When his mate didn't respond, Lorian whispered, "I don't want to hurt you."

"You're not," Randy told him, his strained voice countering his words, even as his scent proclaimed he was telling the truth. Randy smiled at him. "I love the stretch. It was just a bit more than I expected." With a rough chuckle, Randy purred, "You're so damn big, my mate. Love it."

Before Lorian could figure out a response—his brain seemed to stall each time Randy claimed him as his mate—Randy began lowering himself.

As Randy's tight channel swallowed more and more of Lorian's erection, his control of his hips began to slip. His need to rut began clouding his mind, and he desperately wanted to take over. Only his instinct to never hurt his mate kept him in check.

Finally, *finally*, Randy settled his ass on Lorian's groin. He sighed deeply and moaned. Resting one hand behind him on Lorian's knee, Randy moved his other beneath the water.

At first, Lorian thought Randy was going to jack himself. He realized a second later that he wasn't. Instead, Randy was skimming his fingertips around his hole, fondling the stretched skin. At the same time, Randy was scraping his fingernails around the base of Lorian's erection where they were connected.

"Randy," Lorian cried, his balls pulling so tight so fast he thought he would lose it right then. "Fuck!"

"Oh, yeah," Randy replied, his gaze heavy-lidded.

Then Randy returned his hands to Lorian's shoulders. He dug his fingernails into his flesh as he raised himself partway off his cock.

Lorian didn't know how Randy's chute could feel any tighter, but it did. Then the restriction eased as his lover lowered himself back down. When Randy did it a second time, Lorian realized that his mate was controlling his chute muscles.

His control snapping, Lorian spread his legs, planted his feet, and began bucking into his sexy mate. He used his hold on his hips to help speed up Randy's movements, the water hindering their rhythm. It didn't matter, though, because in seconds, Lorian knew he was about to barrel over that edge.

Desperately wanting Randy right there with him, Lorian reached beneath the water and grabbed his lover's prick in a tight grip, drawing a bark of pleasure from him. He squeezed rhythmically as his mate continued to ride him. Growling in bliss, Lorian felt Randy's cock twitch in his hand as Randy cried out his name.

Lorian yanked Randy flush to his body, burying himself deep. His lover shuddered atop him as warmth flooded the space between him. Feeling Randy's chute constrict once more, Lorian stopped fighting it.

Calling Randy's name, Lorian felt his balls draw up. He pumped his seed into his forever love, reveling in marking him on the inside. Needing the same on the outside, Lorian didn't fight it when his canines lengthened, and he sank them deep into the point of Randy's shoulder.

Hot blood poured across his tongue, and he moaned as the rich flavor caused his taste buds to sing. Suckling on Randy's neck, he pulled more into his mouth. At his third swallow, he felt his mate's body jolt, and his lover cried out his name, filling him with smug satisfaction.

A second later, Lorian felt Randy's teeth at his own neck. He hummed in encouragement, then felt the spike of pain. Surprise shot through him, and he tensed. Then the sweetest zings spread across his chest. Lorian's nipples beaded, his gut clenched, and his balls pulled tight once more.

Lorian pulled his teeth free only to tip his head back and bellow Randy's name, his senses blind-sided by one of the most intense orgasms of his life.

When Lorian came back to himself, he spotted the blood dripping down Randy's shoulder. He dipped his head and licked across his mate's flesh, cleaning up the blood and sealing the wound. A new kind of pleasure filled him upon seeing the gorgeous claiming scar on Randy's shoulder, heralding to everyone that the sweet fox shifter was his.

Feeling Randy ease his teeth from his own neck, Lorian smiled. He couldn't wait to see the scar on his throat as he felt his mate lick him clean and seal it. Sighing, Lorian relaxed in the seat, sliding down a little.

With only the barest of encouragement, Randy sprawled over Lorian's body, not even trying to pull free of him.

"Thank you," Lorian whispered, nuzzling Randy's damp hair. "I'm so very blessed."

Randy tipped his head and kissed the underside of Lorian's chin. "I'm pretty sure I'm getting the better end of the deal."

Scoffing, Lorian tilted his head a bit so he could meet Randy's gaze. "And I'm pretty sure that every shifter feels that way about their fated mate."

Smiling, Randy nodded. "I bet so."

Rubbing his palms up and down Randy's lean, wet spine, Lorian sighed with satisfaction. He didn't think anything could ruin the moment.

"Lorian, I'm so very sorry to interrupt." Madison's voice came through the intercom, echoing in the vast space. "But your mother's here."

And I was wrong. What the fuck does she want?

Focusing on Randy, Lorian forced a smile. "Ready to meet my mother?"

Chapter Ten

Randy gaped at Lorian. "What?" He would forever deny the squeak in his voice. "Like *this*?"

Lorian smiled, amusement lighting his dark eyes. "Well, it would serve her right, dropping by unannounced like this"—he waggled his eyebrows for an instant before sobering—"but I was actually thinking of getting dressed first."

Knowing he would have to do it sooner or later—*better get the explosions out of the way sooner, right*—Randy grimaced even as he nodded. "Okay," he whispered.

When Lorian cradled his jaw, Randy lifted his gaze back to meet his eyes, uncertain when he'd even lowered them. While there was a bit of tightness around his eyes, betraying his own unease, he told him, "Listen to me, Randy." Lorian waited a heartbeat, holding his gaze. "*You* are my fated mate. We have claimed each other. There is nothing on this earth that will make me walk away from you. No family. No friends. No job." Resting his forehead on Randy's, Lorian purred, "You're it for me, and I'm not going to let you go, either."

Randy smiled back, his tension easing a little. "Okay." That time he managed to make his words come out a little more firm.

Before Randy could pull away, Lorian dipped his head and captured his mouth. He thrust his tongue between his lips and delved deep for a few seconds. Enjoying the feel of his mate's lips, Randy joined in the tongue-play. To his surprise, his prick even began to plump up.

Groaning, Lorian broke the kiss. He grinned, saying, "You

are so damn irresistible."

When Lorian helped Randy slide off his lap and to his feet, he realized his buffalo shifter was in the same boat as him. Of course, one thought of meeting the man's domineering mother killed it swiftly enough. Randy began moving through the water toward the stairs.

"You still there, Mads?" Lorian called, the swishing of the water telling Randy that he followed.

"Yes, sir. Where would you like—Wait, Misses Bakerman. Where are you going?"

A woman's voice came faintly through the line, and Randy would bet he only noticed it due to his shifter hearing.

"I saw where you were calling, Madison," the woman claimed haughtily. "I'll not wait a second longer."

"Your mother is on her way to the pool," Madison warned. "Sorry, sir."

Lorian growled under his breath for an instant, but none of his ire filled his voice when he replied, "I understand, Madison. Thank you."

"Yes, sir."

Turning to Randy, Lorian ordered, "I guarantee you can't dress your wet body in those jeans in less than five seconds. I'll get you a towel."

"I'm a shifter," Randy reminded him even as he allowed Lorian to pass him in the water. "I'm used to nudity. Isn't your mother?"

Scoffing, Lorian shrugged. "She'll pretend to be scandalized regardless." He touched Randy's shoulder, telling him, "If you really don't want to meet her, you could hide behind the waterfall." Lorian pointed toward it. "There's a small nook behind the sheet of water."

Randy was so damn tempted, and as he watched Lorian exit the water, he even took a few steps in that direction. Then he straightened his back and moved to one of the seats, instead. He had just sat down and Lorian had just pulled open the cabinet containing the towels when a regal-looking woman with gray in her upswept, classy hair-do walked in.

"Lorian Dwight Bakerman, how could you be so crass?"

"Full name," Lorian commented dryly, keeping his back to her. "Must be serious." He began rubbing a towel over his shoulders, back, and ass.

To Randy's surprise, Annabelle didn't look his way, seeming completely oblivious to his presence.

"Care to explain these?"

After wrapping the towel around his waist, Lorian grabbed a second and placed it around his shoulders. Finally, he turned to face his mother. Lorian held out his hand for the tablet she'd pulled from her purse.

Lorian arched one brow. Holding it back out to her, he asked, "It's crass to go to lunch?"

"It's not lunch that's the problem," his mother replied hotly. "It's who you're having it with."

Obviously playing dumb, Lorian quipped, "Councilman Colearian isn't fit company?"

"Don't play dumb with me," Annabelle snapped coldly, grabbing the tablet. She stabbed a red-tipped fingernail at the screen. "*Him.* You are fawning all over some little twink. Is he even a shifter?" Shaking her head, Annabelle shoved the tablet into her purse, then crossed her arms over her breasts. "It doesn't matter. You are never to see him again, and you will never embarrass me in such a way again." Without giving Lorian two seconds to respond, she added, "Did you know Kelly showed up at my afternoon tea party and showed these pictures to everyone there? You'll come to dinner this evening, and you'll be charming and engaging with the ladies there as you laugh off the pictures as a friend who needed help with the menu."

While Randy had never had a close relationship with his mother—even before he'd come out as gay—she had never behaved like this lady. He felt torn. He didn't know if he should go barging in like a flaming queen, or if he should hide beneath the surface of the pool until she was gone.

"Mother, you're out of line." Lorian's voice came out steely with a hard edge.

From the way Annabelle blinked, Randy would bet that was his councilman's voice, and he'd probably rarely, if ever, directed it at her.

Annabelle rallied quickly, though. "Don't you take that tone with me," she ordered, narrowing her eyes at Lorian. "I am your mother, and you wouldn't be where you are without me. You will respect me."

"Mother, I respect you as a shifter," Lorian declared, his tone still hard. Then he whipped the towel off his shoulders and began moving past her. "But I would never deny my mate, and I would never ask another to do so. Mates are gifts from the gods."

"What are—" She gasped. Grabbing Lorian's arm, she tried to stop him, but he kept moving. "What have you done?" Obviously, she'd spotted Randy's claiming mark on Lorian's neck. She snapped her hand from Lorian's bicep, not that he acknowledged it, and lifted it to her throat as she finally realized they weren't alone. With wide eyes, as if seeing the most horrible thing in her life, Annabelle whispered again, "Lorian, what have you done?"

Holding up the towel, Lorian smiled at Randy. "Come on, my mate. Time to dry off."

Randy swallowed hard, then dug deep for courage. Keeping his focus on Lorian's warm, dark eyes, he lifted himself from the pool. Once standing, Randy forced a smile and took the towel.

"Thank you, Lorian," Randy murmured, wrapping it

around his waist. Never had he felt so grateful for a thick, fluffy towel. The fact that Lorian wrapped his arm around his waist helped a whole lot, too.

After pecking a kiss to Randy's temple—which he loved every time he did it—Lorian focused back on Annabelle. "Mother, this is Randy Cullers, my fated mate." Lorian waved his free hand toward his mother. "This is my mother, Annabelle Bakerman."

"No," Annabelle stated flatly. "No, he is not."

Lorian cocked his head. "Mother, I think you need to stop right there." He lifted his hand, palm out. "It's a criminal offense to attempt to keep fated mates apart, and you're walking a dangerous line in that direction."

Annabelle straightened to her full height, which was about an inch taller than Randy's five-foot-ten.

"I see," Annabelle stated, doing her best to look down her nose at them both. "You would turn your back on your heritage and refuse the duty of your name."

"I have absolutely no idea what that's supposed to mean, Mother," Lorian countered. Randy could even scent the confusion and frustration he was trying to keep in check. "I have never turned my back on my ex-herd-mates. If they ever came to me, I would do my best to help them, just as I would any shifter who requested aid."

Narrowing her eyes, Annabelle pinned him with a quelling look, which didn't seem to work, because Lorian just arched one brow at her. Evidently, that wasn't the reaction she'd expected. She blinked once, then went on the offensive again.

"You have claimed this"—she waved her hand toward Randy, a sneer curving her lips—"shifter, so I'm aware you can't get it up for anyone else now. I'll find you a suitable carrier, and we'll use artificial insemination."

Lorian gaped even as his arm tightened around Randy's waist—probably because he'd backed up a step in shock.

"Mother, if Randy and I decide to ever have children"—he paused to look at Randy—"which is *not* a requirement for my life. That's totally up to you"—then he refocused on his mother—"Randy and I will decide on the surrogate at that time."

Once again lifting her chin, Annabelle stated, "So you *are* turning your back on your responsibilities." She narrowed her eyes and used a domineering voice that had probably always gotten her whatever she wanted in the past. "I raised you better than that, Lorian. After everything I've done for you, you owe me this."

"I owe you a grandchild?" Lorian sounded just as confused as Randy felt even as he shook his head. "That's not how motherhood works." Then Lorian frowned. "And why would you start pressuring me for one now?"

Looking at him as if he were the densest person on the planet, Annabelle replied, "Because I'm almost four hundred years old. I need the time in order to train him or her to take your place on the council."

Lorian scoffed, shaking his head again. "This conversation is over, Mother." He looked to the left. "Madison?"

The door instantly opened, and Madison appeared. "Yes, sir?"

"My mother was just leaving." Then Lorian smiled, glancing pointedly at the claiming mark he'd left on Randy's shoulder. "And the pool will need to be cleaned."

Madison's lips twitched, telling Randy that he was doing his damnedest to keep a straight face. "I'll see to it, sir." Then he focused on Annabelle. "If you'll come with me, Misses Bakerman. I will see you out."

Annabelle opened her mouth as if preparing to refuse. Then she cast a cold gaze at Randy before spinning on her heel and heading toward Madison.

Randy wasn't entirely certain, but he thought she hissed,

"You'll be sorry."

After the door closed behind her and Madison, Randy wrapped his arms around Lorian and rested his head on his chest. Lorian returned the embrace, rubbing up and down his back lightly. He even nuzzled his bearded lips against his temple a little, as if he liked how it felt. Randy sure did, so he would never object.

Unable to help himself, Randy finally murmured, "Is that better or worse than how you thought it would go?"

Lorian's chest expanded against Randy's own as he took in a deep breath. "Well." He let it out just as slowly. "It definitely went differently than I thought." Lifting his head, Lorian met Randy's gaze. "And while I didn't scent any deceit from her, I think wanting a grandchild was a complete cover." He frowned. "I don't know what her angle is."

Randy mulled that over for a few seconds before asking, "Did she really say what I thought she said?" When Lorian didn't reply right away, he added, "At the end, when she was leaving. Did you hear, um, anything?"

Tightening his arms, Lorian held Randy close. He tucked his face against his neck and nodded, his forehead sliding over his flesh. Randy continued to hold him, feeling the tension in Lorian's body and knowing that he needed the comfort.

After a few minutes, Lorian lifted his head. "I heard her," he confirmed. After a few seconds of hesitation, he added, "Did you know it's illegal to threaten a member of the council?"

Gaping, Randy shook his head. "Really?"

"While, technically, the law was written in regards to threatening their life, she said something so ambiguous, so open-ended, there's so many ways to interpret it."

Randy had to agree. There was. Maybe she thought she would get leniency because she was his mother? Randy would be the first to admit that he never understood what was going on in a woman's head, no matter the age.

"Does something have to be done about it?" Randy asked curiously.

Sighing, Lorian nodded. "There are procedures. Yes." Then he crossed to a panel on the wall, opened the clear box, and picked up the phone. After pushing several buttons and obviously getting a response, Lorian stated, "Hello, Igor. I'm sorry to have to bother you again today."

Lorian paused a few seconds, a small smile toying around the edges of his lips. "I appreciate that, Igor." Rubbing the back of his neck, he stated into the phone, "I need to order an investigation, an extremely subtle one." Lorian paused only a heartbeat before saying, "My mother."

Grimacing, Lorian nodded. "Yes, I'm serious. She's not at all happy I found my mate and said some things that are . . . questionable." Quickly he added, "It could have just been heat of the moment shit, but this is my mate, and I won't take any chances."

Randy felt himself warm upon hearing those words. As he watched Lorian finish up his call with Igor, he thought about his lover. Earlier, Lorian had been happy and relaxed, and Randy wanted to see that man again.

While Randy couldn't force Lorian's mother to accept their mating with grace, he could do something else—distract.

As soon as Lorian replaced the handset to the cradle and once again closed the box, Randy called Lorian's name. His mate turned, and Randy dropped the towel. He then turned, bent provocatively, and picked up the set-aside bottle of lube.

After Randy had straightened, a glance over his shoulder told him he had Lorian's full attention. "Come swimming," he purred, then dove into the water.

To Randy's pleasure, even as he swam under water, he heard a second splash not far behind him.

Chapter Eleven

Lorian glared at Igor. "Would you repeat that?"

It took every bit of self-control he had not to tighten his arm around Randy's waist. If this news sent his mate running, he would murder that woman—mother or not.

"Your wedding date to Demona Rinaldi is on July twenty-nineth."

Okay. So the information didn't change.

Peering down at Randy, Lorian could only say, "I never agreed to marry Demona, and I sure as hell never proposed to her."

To Lorian's utter relief, Randy snorted as he rolled his eyes. "I lived in a little skulk in Massachusetts, and we didn't even try to use arranged marriages." He frowned up at Lorian. "What's Demona's animal? Maybe I can crash your wedding and scratch her eyes out."

Lorian smiled at his suddenly fierce mate. Over the last couple of weeks, Randy had truly begun to come into his own. He'd renovated several of their private rooms, hosted a couple of barbeques for their friends, and he'd even become a popular visitor at Shifter Headquarters. In fact, several of those working there had purchased some of Randy's creations, others ordering even more. His mate was truly making a home for himself with him.

Should have known better than to think this would send him running.

"Unfortunately, she's a buffalo, too, my mate," Lorian told him with a fond smile directed his way. "Not the best idea."

"Damn." Randy crossed his arms over his chest and pretended to pout. That only lasted a second before he brightened and stated, "Okay, I'll put a pillow under my shirt, then come running in at the *I object* part, and tell everyone that you already knocked me up."

Barking a laugh, Lorian cuddled Randy close to him. He noticed that even the normally stoic Igor sported a smile—albeit, a small one. Lorian had always appreciated the Russian wolf shifter's dedication, but he appreciated Dakota's sense of humor, too.

Sighing dramatically, Randy lifted his hand and flopped it in the air. "Well, I'm out of ideas," he claimed breezily. "Anyone else?"

Lorian appreciated Randy's response, although he could feel the tension running through his mate's body. He wasn't as relaxed about it as he let on.

"I have an idea, though," Lorian stated. "I'll go to Demona's house and tell her there is no wedding, and I won't be showing up."

"I would advise against that," Igor immediately stated.

Narrowing his eyes, Lorian pinned his gaze on the enforcer. "Why." He saw the anger simmering in the male's gray eyes and growled. "There's more. What is it?"

Randy raised his hand. "And how did you find out about this wedding, anyway?" He scowled, annoyance filling his scent. "You'd think someone would have leaked something like that somewhere before now."

"I sent Investigator Stigg in undercover," Igor explained, answering Randy's question first. "He was in between assignments, and I didn't think it would take him long to get into your mother's good graces, and I was right."

Lorian scoffed, nodding. Upon seeing Randy's questioning look, he explained, "Paul Stiggard is a brown bear shifter that used to be friends with a couple of enforcers who went rogue.

Everyone actually thought that he was a spy for them, but he was cleared." When Randy still appeared confused, Lorian added, "He's also a favorite of our resident councilman bigot, Peregrine, so of course, my mother would assume he's of a like mind."

"But he's not?" Randy questioned.

Igor actually scoffed, a chuckle escaping him. "No. He's oh-so-gay, not that very many people know it."

Randy immediately nodded and lifted his fingers to his lips, miming locking them and throwing away the key.

Lorian pecked Randy's cheek, loving how his fox had brought some levity to what had been a drab and boring life.

"Well, in two days, your mother is going to allow the news to leak." Igor made air quotes. "She expects you to come running, and when you do, she's going to lock you up." His attention turning to Randy, Igor stated, "Then she's going to kidnap Randy and use that to force you to agree to the wedding."

"What the hell is the point, though?" Randy asked, sounding confused. "It's not like he can knock Demona up. He's bonded."

"That's where kidnapping you comes in," Igor told them, his lips twisting in distaste. "They intend to use a mixture of drugs and Randy's pheromones to get you hard, Councilman." His gaze shifted to the wall over their head, and his tone sounded cold. "Then your seed will be collected, and Demona will be artificially inseminated."

Lorian snarled under his breath as he glared at Igor. "So they intend to rape me."

"Yes, Councilman."

"Not happening," Randy declared, snarling.

"No, it's not," Igor agreed. His smirk turned cruel. "Because if you don't show up like your mother thinks you will, they'll be sending Stigg to get you."

"Stigg?" Lorian shook his head. "Really?"

Igor nodded. "They think that because he's a council enforcer, that he'll be able to get close to you." Cracking his knuckles, Igor growled, "Instead, he's a spy for us. He'll keep us posted on what's going on."

"Gods, my own mother," Lorian grumbled. "I knew she was controlling and manipulative, but never would I have thought she'd stoop to something like this." It really didn't make sense to him. "Why?"

Wincing, Igor cleared his throat. He shifted in his seat, appearing distinctly uncomfortable.

Even knowing another shoe was about to drop, Lorian asked, "What?"

"She owes Demona's family money," Igor revealed, shaking his head. "A *lot* of money. Getting Demona as your spouse, the wife of a councilman, was supposed to bail her out. Instead, you mated." He waved toward Randy. With a shrug, Igor added, "They've settled on a child, instead, so that way, they can have a son on the council before too long." He leveled a hard look Lorian's way. "They'll also use the child as leverage to get you to do as they wish. Voting and such."

"Gods, it would probably work, too," Lorian admitted, disturbed that his mother knew him so well. "Of course I'd want to do anything for my offspring."

Randy rubbed his palm over Lorian's chest, helping to soothe him. "Well, now we know the plan and can stop it," he murmured, cuddling close to his side. "And when we do decide to have kids someday, she's *never* babysitting."

Lorian chuckled softly, appreciating that his mate could make him laugh at such a time. Then he actually processed what Randy had said. He snapped his focus to his mate's face and sniffed, trying to decide how serious he was.

"What?" Randy scowled at him. "What'd I say?"

"Do you want kids someday?"

Randy opened his mouth, then snapped it shut just as quickly. "Um." Hunching his shoulders, he nibbled his bottom lip.

Lifting a hand to Randy's jaw, Lorian gently tugged his bottom lip free of his teeth. Although his mate didn't censor his words very often anymore, breaking the habit was still a work in progress. One of Lorian's favorite ways to pull his lip free was with his own mouth, but he figured that, since the move normally led to sex, he shouldn't start that with Igor in the room.

"Um?" Lorian pressed gently.

"I-I . . . I don't actually know," Randy admitted with a shrug. "I've truly never thought about it. The babysitter comment just sort of, um, came out."

Lorian chuckled softly as he nodded. "That's an honest answer, my mate." Nuzzling Randy's temple, he crooned, "We'll discuss it again in a few years if you want. I'd like a couple of decades with just you first."

"It's a deal," Randy replied, happiness filling his scent.

Igor rose. "When I hear more from Stigg, I'll let you know, Councilman."

Peering up at the large wolf shifter, Lorian offered, "You could call me Lorian when we're alone, you know."

His lips curving into a small smile, Igor told him, "Your offer honors me."

After the enforcer had left, Lorian realized Igor hadn't actually agreed.

Just as Igor had warned, three days later, rumors began circulating about Councilman Lorian Bakerman marrying Demona Rinaldi. To Lorian's surprise, it was Desmond, the chef, who approached him first. After giving him the anchovies for his grilled chicken Caesar salad, he shifted from foot to foot in obvious uncertainty.

"Hi, Desmond," Lorian greeted with a smile. "Thank you for keeping these in stock. I truly appreciate it."

"C-Can I ask you, um, something, Councilman Lorian?" Desmond began slowly, twisting his hands before him.

"Of course."

Lorian focused on the fox shifter. Idly, he wondered if Desmond's fox looked anything like Randy's pretty red animal. He'd loved playing in animal form every time Randy had coaxed him into taking time to run around outside.

I really hadn't been doing that enough.

"Well, sir." Desmond glanced around, obviously checking to see who was around. The only other person at the table was Dakota, and the cafeteria was almost empty.

"You can speak freely, Desmond," Lorian encouraged.

Desmond nodded. "Well, you've been introducing Randy as your mate for the last couple of weeks."

Lorian nodded, suddenly realizing what Desmond was obviously trying to work up the courage to talk about. Even already knowing, he had to play dumb.

"Of course." Lorian grinned widely, the move not hard when he thought of his mate. "I've been truly blessed by Fate. Randy is an amazing man."

That must have been what Desmond needed, for he blurted in a rush, "Then why are you marrying some woman named Demona on the twenty-nineth?"

Lorian blinked, doing his best to feign confusion. "I'm sorry." He frowned. "Marry who, when?"

Desmond frowned. "I heard Bart talking about it earlier today," he stated, referring to another shifter who worked in the kitchens. "He said that Karissa on the cleaning staff heard from Spike in maintenance who heard it from"—Desmond frowned, pausing—"I'm not sure who, but you're supposed to be marrying a woman named Demona on the twenty-nineth. Everyone is wondering why you're claiming to have found your fated mate if you're getting married." Hugging himself, Desmond stared at the floor as he mumbled, "It doesn't, uh, you know, um, p-put you i-in a very g-good light."

"You're right, Desmond," Lorian replied softly. Furrowing his brows, he rested his palms on the table and tapped his forefingers restlessly. "I appreciate you bringing this to my attention. Truly, I do."

Desmond snapped his focus back to him. "S-So you're not, uh, getting married?"

"No," Lorian immediately replied. "At least, not to Demona." Smiling a little, he mused, "I wonder if Randy would like to get married."

There's an idea. Marry Randy first. Damn, I like that idea. Why didn't I think of that before?

Lorian decided to propose the idea to Randy as soon as he arrived home.

Propose. Ha-ha.

Turning to Dakota, Lorian asked, "Have you heard any rumors about my impending nuptials?"

Dakota shook his head. "No, Councilman, but I'll start asking around." His smile appeared hard. "I'll start with those people that you mentioned, Desmond."

"Thank you." Lorian turned back to Desmond. "And thanks to you, too, Desmond. I don't know who's spreading the rumors"—which was true, from a certain point of view—"but I'll definitely be dealing with them." With a smile, Lorian added, "And I'll definitely be sending a message council-wide to correct the inaccuracy shortly."

Lorian figured that would be the best way to get a rumor back to his mother—completely deny the wedding plans and announce to every shifter in their system that he was mated with Randy.

Hope that doesn't paint a target on Randy's back.

Seeing as Dane was with Randy right then, since Dakota was with Lorian, he knew his mate would be just fine.

After Desmond walked away, Lorian turned to Dakota. He leaned close to the man and murmured, "That was interesting."

Dakota nodded. "Damn ballsy of Des. Didn't know he had it in him."

"Me, neither." Lorian appreciated it, though. "Let's take our meal to go. It would look more normal."

"Definitely." Dakota began placing their plates on a tray. "Let's go."

Lorian rose, picked up his bottle of iced tea, and followed Dakota from the cafeteria. As he returned to his office, he passed a number of shifters in the hallways. It was easy to tell which ones had heard the rumor and which ones had not. Those who'd heard gave him funny looks, cut their gaze away from him, or stared at him covertly.

If Lorian hadn't been aware of what was truly going on, he would have been genuinely upset by the behavior. He knew that had been his mother's plan, too. She wanted him upset enough to confront her.

Not on your terms, bitch.

Fighting back a cringe at his thoughts, Lorian headed to his office. Then he put together a quick email about the rumors and how they weren't true. He then touted his love for Randy, how proud he was to be mated with him, and how he couldn't be happier. Lorian also asked for help in identifying the perpetrator of the lies being spread about him.

After sending it to everyone in the directory, Lorian ate his mid-afternoon meal. He shot a quick text to Randy, too, telling him that someone had confronted him regarding the rumors. His mate had responded with heart emojis and how much he'd loved the email, which Dane had already shown him.

Lorian had smiled and returned to his food.

It hadn't taken long for phone calls and emails to start

pouring in. A few people expressed their outrage that someone would spread such vulgar lies about him and promised that they would let him know if they heard anything. Some expressed their sympathy that someone was doing that to him. Then there were a couple who called him an asshole for leading Demona on like that, only to walk away from her a week or so before the wedding.

"Damn, some people are real assholes," Dakota muttered, reading over his shoulder. He jotted down their names. "Let's make certain these guys aren't more involved."

"Good idea."

Lorian didn't get a whole lot of work done that day, but at least their plan to thwart his mother had started moving forward.

At four-thirty, Lorian called it a day, more than ready to get home. When he pulled into his driveway, his gut tightened.

"What the hell is my mother's limo doing in my driveway?" Lorian snarled. "And why wasn't I called?"

"Don't know. Dane should have—Shit!" Dakota snarled. "Signal jammer. No calls in or out."

Lorian growled in anger. "If she's harmed one hair on Randy's head, I will end her." Even before Dakota had stopped the car, he was unlocking the door and pushing out of the vehicle.

Dakota barely managed to catch Lorian before he yanked open the front door. "Wait a second," the enforcer ordered, ignoring Lorian's warning snarl. Shaking him once, Dakota ordered gruffly, "Listen, Lorian. You can't go in there half-cocked. We have to be careful." Holding his gaze levelly, Dakota warned, "We don't know how many people she brought with her in that limo."

Realizing Dakota was right didn't make it any easier to stay his instinct to race inside to find his mate.

Still, Lorian did it.

"What's the plan?"

Dakota pinned him with a grim smile as he handed Lorian a tranquilizer gun that he'd had hidden who knew where. "Do not leave my side," he ordered. "Not for anything."

Even as Lorian made that promise, he wondered if he could keep it.

Chapter Twelve

"Oh, damn," Dane commented, leaning over Randy's shoulder. "That's really pretty. How do you decide on the colors?"

"Thanks." Randy flashed a smile the Komodo dragon shifter's way. "But I can't take credit this time around. Lolita asked for six eight-by-eight-inch pillows with a diamond pattern in her wedding colors."

"Who's Lolita?" the enforcer asked curiously as he rounded the chair and sat in another, stretching his long legs out before him.

Randy arched one brow as he glanced Dane's way before refocusing on his work. "Lolita works in the Shifter Council's kitchens," he told him. "She's getting married in September, and she wants to give these to her bridesmaids as gifts. I'll sew a ribbon in the middle of the pattern of each pillow. That way, she can tie a unique charm onto each one for each bridesmaid."

"Damn," Dane murmured. "Six bridesmaids."

Out of the corner of Randy's eye, he noticed the way the large shifter shook his head. Chuckling, he asked, "What?"

"Is six normal?" Dane questioned. "That seems like a lot."

While Randy really didn't know the answer to that, he grinned anyway and teased, "I thought big wedding parties were the norm down here in the south."

Dane snorted. "Hell if I know. I don't remember the last time I went to a shifter wedding," he told him. "And we don't interact on a personal level with too many humans due to the aging thing."

Randy nodded, understanding. Shifters could live upward of five centuries, which made having close friendships with humans who didn't know about the paranormal world extremely difficult. They were constantly having to recreate their identities, which meant leaving those they cared about behind.

"Well, this party is five bridesmaids," Randy admitted. "The sixth pillow is for the flower girl."

"How long do you think it takes you to make each of those pillows?" Dane asked curiously.

"Oh, maybe a week to cut all the pieces and a week for sewing each one," Randy told him, pleased at his interest and happy that the shifter didn't poo-poo his chosen hobby-turned-profession.

While Randy knew he didn't actually need to make money, he had to do something with his time. Sewing blankets and pillows and other tchotchkes, taking on-demand orders via word of mouth and the internet, Randy filled his time by doing what he enjoyed.

"That's impressive," Dane commented, sounding the same. "I can't imagine—"

A chime on Dane's phone interrupted him. He pulled his phone from his belt and scowled at the screen. A second later, a low growl escaped his throat.

"We may have a problem," Dane stated. "Best wrap that up for a few minutes until we figure out what's what."

Randy quickly did as he'd been told. After finishing the stitch he'd been pulling, he slid the needle through a seam so he didn't leave any holes behind. He settled the project in his basket on the end table before standing and crossing to Dane, who was tapping on his phone and rising to his feet.

"What's going on?" Randy didn't like the lines of worry on the big enforcer's face.

Dane held up his phone. "No service." He crossed to the intercom, which was installed in many rooms of the massive estate home. Pushing a button, Dane called, "Emelio. You in the kitchen, man?"

After a few seconds, a Spanish-accented man replied, "*Si, señor*. How may I help you?"

"Do you have service on your phone, Emilio?" Dane asked.

"My phone? I check."

While Emelio sounded confused, he must have been doing as Dane asked, because there was silence for a few seconds. The man kept his phone on the counter near the oven, using it to play music. Then Emelio's voice returned, sounding worried.

"No, *señor*. No bars."

"Yeah, me, neither," Dane revealed. "Be careful down there. Okay?"

Everyone working for a councilman knew there were dangers involved. "*Si, señor*."

After closing the connection, Dane contacted the security office. "Pinky, why are the cells down?"

"Cameras are down, too." Pinky told them the disturbing news. "I was just rebooting to see if it was a glitch."

"You get those often?" Dane asked dryly.

That timing sounded way too coincidental for Randy's tastes.

"Never," Pinky replied. "And I have a back-up alert system that's telling me the front gate just opened."

"Son of a bitch," Dane snapped. "Stay sharp down there."

Pinky snorted, then the line went dead.

Dane rolled his eyes. "Yeah, that was probably a stupid thing to say to him."

"What do you mean?" Randy asked, following Dane to the window, which faced the front lawn. Just as Dakota had shown him weeks before, he stayed on one side of the window to look out.

Dane did the same on the other side. "Well," Dane drawled, his focus outside. "You ever hear why he's called Pinky?"

Randy shook his head. He'd thought it odd, but he hadn't had the courage to ask. Seeing as he didn't know the wiry, sort of reclusive, mountain goat shifter very well, yet, Randy didn't think it was any of his business, either.

"He's an expert in a number of forms of martial arts," Dane told him even as he tipped his head to the side. His voice became vacant as he stated, "Some say that he can kill his opponent with just his pinky, hence the name."

"Seriously?" Randy squeaked. "Glad he's on our side."

Grinning at him, Dane nodded once. "Yup." When he returned his focus to the window, he growled low in his throat. "What the fuck are you doing here?"

"Who?" Randy wondered what he was seeing. "What's going on?"

"Annabelle is here," Dane told him, still staring out the window. "And four men just went around the place, a pair in each direction, while two more are accompanying her to the door." Shaking his head, Dane mumbled, "I don't see Stigg. They must have left him out of the loop."

"He wouldn't betray us, would he?" Randy asked. He'd only met the shifter once, and he'd been intense.

Dane pinned Randy with a serious gaze. "Absolutely not, Randy," he assured. "Absolutely not. He's one of us."

Randy nodded, having to believe the man.

"We're going to stand in the hall and eavesdrop for a second," Dane told him, beckoning him. With his brows furrowed in a hard line, he added, "If trouble starts, and I think it will, you go into your bedroom and hide. Do you understand? You're not to fight unless it's a last resort."

"I told you I wanted one of those tranquilizer guns that Theo had," Randy grumbled. No one had given him lessons, yet, though.

"After this, I'll remind Lorian," Dane assured him. "Now promise."

Randy nodded, sticking close to Dane's side. "Promise." His fox yipped worriedly in his mind. He agreed with his animal and Dane.

Nothing good would come of Annabelle's visit.

They'd crept halfway down the hall toward the central hall when Annabelle's distinctive voice carried to them. "You can bring Randy to me, Madison, or my friends will find him for me." Her voice hardened. "You won't like that option."

"Misses Bakerman," Madison replied, a growl in his voice. "I would never betray my councilman by handing over his mate to you. You'll have to kill me first."

"Actually, I don't," Annabelle replied loftily.

A second later, Madison roared. The tell-tale sound of shifting filled the air, as did feminine laughter.

Dane grabbed Randy's upper arm and hurried him back down the hall. They hadn't even made it to the bedroom door when they heard the sound of heavy steps pounding up the stairs. Reaching beyond Randy, Dane opened the door and pushed him inside, following him.

"You need to hide," Dane ordered him. "I'll take them out or go down trying."

"Don't say that," Randy hissed, even as he began hurrying across the room. "I don't want you injured because of me."

"This is my job, Randy. It's what I do." Dane met his gaze squarely. "You're my friend as well as my charge. Don't get involved."

"Then promise to stay alive," Randy insisted, not able to bear the idea that his friend would die for him, job or not.

"Without knowing what kind of shifters Annabelle

brought with her or if she brought any firepower, I can't do that," Dane told him even as he stripped his shirt from his body. With a wink, he added, "But don't worry. I'm pretty damn good at what I do, and I have every intention of sticking around so I can meet my own mate." Dane began shoving his jeans off next, then paused. "Remember, there are more bad guys creeping around the place. Don't leave your hiding place for anyone you don't know."

Once Randy nodded, Dane began to shift.

Randy had never seen the enforcer's animal, although he'd known he was big. Even in his and Lorian's huge bedroom, the male quickly took up the majority of the space. Within seconds, one huge slitted eye blinked at him before focusing on the bedroom door.

Hearing the bang of what was probably a shoulder against a door, Randy did as he was told—he ran and hid. He ducked into the bathroom, closing the door behind him. Randy locked it for good measure, although he doubted that would help at all, especially when he heard the crack of the outer door followed by the thud of it slamming into the doorstop.

"Holy shit," a male voice shouted. "Fire, fire, fire."

Dane's distinctive hissing roar echoed through the door. There were gunshots followed by thuds and yells and screams. The crunch of furniture was followed by something cracking as well as a heavy thud that worried Randy.

Finally, silence fell. Randy wrapped his arms around his torso, straining his ears for any hint of noise. When he made out labored breathing, he was so tempted to open the bathroom door and see what had happened.

Only his promise to run and hide kept him inside there.

Good thing, too.

The thump of footsteps reached Randy, giving him hope. That was quickly dashed by a stranger calling, "Lloyd?"

A second later, another man muttered, "Holy shit."

"The enforcer is still alive," the first man claimed.

"He won't be for long," the second man stated, a hard edge to his voice.

"Skip the enforcer," Annabelle ordered. "I don't give a fuck about him."

"But he killed Lloyd and Harry," the second man's voice replied angrily.

"Find the fox," Annabelle practically screamed.

Knowing it wouldn't be long until one of the men with Annabelle would break down his door, Randy turned to the linen cupboard. He found the catch and opened the secret door to the tunnel. Slipping inside onto the small platform, Randy quickly closed the door, all the while praying that Dane would be okay.

Randy hurried down the spiral staircase as silently as possible. Pausing at the bottom, he peeked through the peephole. When Randy had asked Lorian why it was there, with a laugh, he'd explained that he didn't want to surprise someone *in flagrante delecto.*

Thankful for Lorian's foresight, Randy watched and waited. Just as he was about to open the door, he spotted a shadow, so he waited some more. A few seconds later, a man he didn't recognize strode through the pool room, pausing to survey the area for several minutes.

Randy waited another five minutes after the man had left before finally easing the door open. After a quick glance around, he closed the door, stripped, and stuffed his clothes in the cupboard. Finally, he shifted.

As soon as Randy felt stable on his paws, he skittered across the slick tile and trotted down the steps into the pool. He swam as swiftly as possible to the waterfall. It took a couple of tries in his canine form, but he managed to clamber up the rocks and into the small grotto Lorian had told him about that first day.

With his fur keeping him warm, Randy knew he could hide in there for days before hunger and thirst would drive him out.

Curling up, with his tail over his nose as he strained to see through the falling curtain, Randy did as he'd promised.

He hid.

EPILOGUE

"Where the fuck is he?" Lorian roared, tugging at his hair. "Did they manage to lie?" His gut clenched at the idea. "Was Randy taken?"

"No, absolutely not," Stigg assured.

The shifter had shown up only a few minutes after Lorian and Dakota had. He'd apologized that he hadn't been able to warn them. The only reason he'd learned about it was because the shifter female he'd been *dating* had been angry about Lorian's email. She'd called him to vent.

Stigg had explained that as soon as he'd realized what was happening, he'd hopped in his vehicle and headed that way. It had taken another ten minutes to get her off the phone. Then he'd tried to call Dane, but it had gone straight to voicemail. His next call had been to Dakota, which had also gone to voicemail, since they'd left work early and had already arrived. Stigg had shown up a few minutes later, just as Pinky had figured out how to disarm the jammer that had been in their vehicle.

"If they'd managed to kidnap him, that bitch would already be calling to gloat." Stigg growled under his breath, his lips curling as a shudder went through his big body. "I can't wait to break it off with her."

"We'll find him," Dakota vowed, gripping Lorian's shoulder.

Lorian took a deep breath as he nodded. Meeting the man's green eyes, he asked, "Shouldn't you have gone with your brother?"

Dane had been shot multiple times, and while unconscious, his thick hide had saved him. Their bedroom, however . . . that was in shambles. Everything would have to be gutted.

Dakota shook his head. "Del and Miggs are with him. I'll go after we find Randy."

"Thank you," Lorian muttered, knowing he would be totally losing his shit without the friendly enforcer's calming presence.

"Okay, so we know a battle took place in the bedroom," Stigg pointed out. "Let's start there." He began climbing the stairs. "If Dane did battle in here, then he was protecting Randy."

Nodding, Dakota stopped inside the destroyed room's door. "But we don't smell any of Randy's blood, so we know he wasn't injured." Then he frowned and turned to face Lorian. "Dane would have told him to run and hide. Where would Randy hide?"

"The bathroom," Lorian whispered.

"But it's a dead-end," Stigg pointed out. "Wouldn't he have gone into the closet? Your back stairway connects there."

Lorian smiled a bit, hope filling him. "That's what most people would assume, but my man is smart." He headed toward the bathroom and strode inside. "This isn't a dead-end." Lorian opened the hidden linen cabinet door and started down the stairs.

"Well, well," Dakota rumbled, following him. "Isn't your house full of surprises?"

"There are a few," Lorian replied, glancing behind and up, spotting Stigg with them. "Don't tell, now."

Stigg snorted, while Dakota grinned.

Reaching the bottom, Lorian checked the peephole. He inhaled deeply and nearly moaned in relief. His mate's scent hung heavy in the small space, telling him his lover had stood there for some time.

Lorian opened the door and did his best to follow the scent, but neither he nor his animal were good at tracking. Instead, he tried to put himself in his mate's mindset. Where would a fox feel safe?

A den. Foxes hole up in dens.

Where's a den?

Sweeping his gaze over the spacious room, Lorian tried to think. His gaze fell on the waterfall, and he remembered his first time with his sweet mate, holding him in the water and—

Waterfall. Grotto behind it.

Lorian sprinted and lunged, ignoring the fact that he still sported a suit and dress shoes. Swimming strongly across the surface, he reached the falls in seconds. Then he gripped the rock surface and pushed up, easing halfway under the waterfall until his head broke through.

There, Lorian found himself face to face with a pair of wide golden-hazel eyes.

"Oh, Randy," Lorian crooned, his voice hitching. "You are way too good at hide and seek, my mate." Resting his weight on one hand, he held out the other and rested it on his fox's head, rubbing one big ear. "Come out, please. I've been so damn worried about you."

In the next instant, Lorian tumbled backward, his arms full of wriggling, licking, yipping fox. He held his mate close and nuzzled his face into his fur as he made his way back to the pool's edge. Still, drenched and fully clothed, Lorian couldn't release his man, yet.

"Shift, my mate," Lorian urged. "Let me see that you're okay."

While Lorian couldn't feel any injuries through his thick wet fur, he needed to be sure. To his relief, before too long, he held his slender naked lover within his arms.

"Oh, Randy," Lorian said on a moan, burying his face in

the crook of his neck. He breathed in his scent for a few seconds, helping to calm his racing heart. "Are you well, my mate?"

"I'm okay," Randy told him, clinging to him with arms and legs. "Is Dane okay? What about Madison? Are they okay?"

"They will be," Lorian assured, touched that his mate's first concern was for his people. "It'll take a little while. They're both in the hospital, but they'll be fine in time."

"Okay. Okay. Good," Randy whispered. He tipped his head up and met his gaze. "He told me to run and hide. He made me promise, so I did."

Lorian nodded. "He's a great man and an amazing enforcer." With a warm smile, he peered Dakota's way, who was grinning like an idiot where he stood at the side of his pool. "Tell him I owe him a debt, and we'll come to see him soon."

Dakota barked a laugh and shook his head. "I'll tell him, but I guarantee he'll say it was just his job." He shrugged and smirked. "Or maybe his honor or some variation of that." After that, Dakota started toward the door. "Good to see you well, Randy. We'll spread the word that he's alive, well, and to give you a little while."

Stigg hummed a bit as he nodded. "I'm glad you're well, little fox." He turned and followed Dakota.

Feeling his lover's naked body in his arms as well as his animal's driving need to reconnect with his lover, Lorian eased Randy down only to peel off his jacket. He remembered at the last minute to pull the single-use packet of lube out of the inside pocket before he tossed the sopping fabric onto the pool's edge. Lorian always carried them, since he never knew when Randy would pop into headquarters to surprise him.

"Wait, what about your mother?"

Even as Randy said to wait, he was unbuttoning and unzipping Lorian's slacks, clearly just as eager.

"She'll most likely be put to death," Lorian admitted as he pulled his button-down from his waistband, giving Randy more room. "But I won't be a part of that decision, for obvious reasons."

After everything she'd attempted, while Lorian felt sadness, he also understood and accepted that she'd brought it on herself, too. She'd made her decision and would pay for it.

Randy froze, staring up at him. "Really?"

Lorian nodded once. "She came between fated mates. That carries a death penalty, and she knew it." Gripping Randy's hands between his own, he brought them to his lips and kissed his knuckles. "Now, no more talk of her. I'm overdressed. Will you help me with that, my mate?"

Smiling, Randy replied, "Oh, yes."

"Good." Lorian watched as Randy reached for his fly again. "Because I need to be naked so I can fuck you under that waterfall."

Randy groaned and nodded vigorously. "Yessss," he hissed and hurried up.

In less than a minute, Lorian was naked, so he grabbed Randy, the lube, and hurried to the waterfall.

About the Author

Charlie started writing fantasy when she was eight, and after stumbling onto her first erotic romance at age nineteen, she realized her true calling. She now focuses on writing gay erotic romance, normally of the paranormal variety, with heroes of all kinds. With the help and support of her husband, Charlie finally fulfilled one of her life-long goals . . . move to acreage with her horses. You can often find her curled up with her laptop and a cup of tea or glass of wine, creating her next adventure. Charlie enjoys exploring the mountains of her new Oregon home on horseback, 4-wheeler, or motorcycle.

She can be reached at ch.richards2010@yahoo.com
Or visit her at www.charlie-richards.com

www.ingramcontent.com/pod-product-compliance
Lightning Source LLC
Chambersburg PA
CBHW070756120626
46557CB00002B/627

* 9 7 8 1 4 8 7 4 3 3 5 4 3 *